She hesitated, moonlight playing over her dusky skin.

"The way you're looking right now, Dave...I'm not so sure if you're the harmless guy I assumed you were. You are a good guy, aren't you?"

He nodded, hoping she'd see the type of man he yearned to be. A guy who didn't twist people's lives around to suit his own needs. A guy who deserved to be a favorite son again, once he returned to his family.

And because he wanted to earn that so much, he lowered his hand, intending to help her into the car and go on his merry way.

But before he could manage that, she stood on her tiptoes, catching his mouth with hers.

Dear Reader,

When I began plotting a new miniseries, I wanted to write about "urban tribes." You know what I mean—the buddies on *Friends* are an example, and they showed us how singletons who live away from their families bond with each other, depend upon each other and, finally, love each other.

From that idea came The Suds Club. Here, in this Laundromat, you'll meet another urban tribe, and the first to fall in love are Naomi Shannon and David Chandler. Some of you might recall David from a previous book, *The Playboy Takes a Wife*. He's a man who's hungering for redemption, but it's only when he makes an accidental stop in The Suds Club that he finds a glimmer of what he's looking for in sweet, kind Naomi.

I hope you'll read the following books, as well!

Here's to your own happy endings....

Crystal Green
www.crystal-green.com

MOMMY AND THE MILLIONAIRE

CRYSTAL GREEN

Published by Silhouette Books

America's Publisher of Contemporary Romance

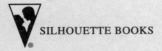

SILHOUETTE BOOKS

ISBN-13: 978-0-373-24887-2
ISBN-10:   0-373-24887-3

MOMMY AND THE MILLIONAIRE

CRYSTAL GREEN

lives near Las Vegas, Nevada, where she writes for the Silhouette Special Edition and Harlequin Blaze lines. She loves to read, overanalyze movies, do yoga and write about her travels and obsessions on her Web site, www.crystal-green.com. There, you can read about her trips on Route 66, as well as her visits to Japan and Italy.

She'd love to hear from her readers by e-mail through the Contact Crystal feature on her Web page!

To my Kentucky Girls… Friends forever.

Chapter One

When the man with the blazing tomato stain on his shirt entered The Suds Club Laundromat, Naomi Shannon was sitting by the dryer and paging through a community college catalog.

The bell on the door went ding and—*boom!*—there he was.

Or maybe a better way of saying it was—*boom!*—there he calmly exploded.

It wasn't really that he seemed "dangerous" as he headed straight for the detergent dispenser. He just had a very smooth method of looking fit to be tied, if she said so herself. The way he moved—so assured, so confident—caught her eye because he basically commanded the room without even trying.

But what *didn't* catch the eye about him?

As he stood in front of the ancient dispenser and

rested his hands on his hips like an admiral inspecting a wrecked ship, Naomi told herself to stop staring. It wasn't polite, first of all, and, most importantly of all, it wasn't on her list of things to do.

Yet…she couldn't help herself.

Dark-blond hair cut in a conservative, neat style. New-looking jeans and a crisp, light-blue button-down that matched his piercing eyes. Work boots that seemed fresh, too. He was slender, but strong and muscular, the veins in his arms etching the surface of his tanned skin. A muscle clenched and ticked near his jaw but, for all her close scrutiny, he still managed to seem as collected as rain in a bucket.

Not that Naomi was a rocket scientist, but she could guess why he might be a bit put out and also why he was in a Laundromat. The nasty red stain on his otherwise perfect shirt did a lot of explaining.

She kept her eyes on him. He was taking a long time to look at that machine, enough time for her skin to get a few goose bumps….

Stop staring.

Shaking her head, she went back to her college catalog, inspecting the accounting classes with double the focus.

Bomp, bomp, bomp, went her clothes in the dryer. The cadence echoed her heartbeat.

But Naomi hadn't traveled nearly cross-country from Kane's Crossing, Kentucky, here to Placid Valley on the outskirts of San Francisco, to get caught up in a man again. Lord knows she had enough male trouble to deal with already.

On the TV, the theme song from *Flamingo Beach* filtered through the detergent-laden air, and Naomi's glance shot toward the screen. Finally, time for her soap. She wasn't going to look at the stranger again. There were better things to take in.

Across the room, the usual crowd had gathered below the tube, which was bolted to the corner of the wall near the ceiling. Though fairly new in town, Naomi had already gotten to know some of the women. Whether they had TVs and washers in their apartments or not, there were about ten people who met on and off here every weekday to watch the soap together and, little by little, they'd made her feel like a part of their group. Today there were only about six other diehards present, all doing their laundry.

Friends, she thought. *It's nice to have some in this new town.*

Then she corrected herself, skimming her hand over her still-flat belly. *Not to say we can't make it on our own.*

She patted the place where her baby was growing, then went back to watching TV, all the while knowing that the stranger with the tomato stain was still behind her. She felt his presence with every rogue tingle buzzing up the skin of her neck.

But then, as *Flamingo Beach* went to commercials before the drama really began, a blond woman madly stuffing the last of her darks into a dryer called to Naomi.

"We've got plenty of seats over here." After finishing her task, she motioned for Naomi to join them while walking to her own chair, sitting and crossing one long leg over the other, then smoothing down the skirt of her smart pink dress.

It was Jenny Hunter's work-from-home day, and the businesswoman was washing a load while taking lunch hour here in this neighborhood gathering spot. She always told Naomi that it got lonely working alone in her apartment every Wednesday. She missed hearing people around, missed the distracting bustle of her office in the city proper.

Naomi closed her catalog. "Coming."

Still, she hesitated all the same, feeling it necessary to glance at the lately arrived food-splattered newcomer again.

He was fighting with a stubborn lever on the dispenser now, his jaw so tight she thought it might shatter. But before that could happen, he stepped back, waited as if to gather his composure, then assessed the temperamental gadget. It was almost as if he were strategizing.

But a new voice interrupted the lovely reverie.

"Naomi? The show's going to start."

When she glanced at the speaker, she found a calmly amused woman easing to a chair in front of the TV, her arms full of laundry consisting mainly of little girls' dresses. Her name was Mei, and she was originally from Hong Kong, though she'd been raised in San Francisco since her mid teens. Long black hair, creamy skin and a strong maternal glow gave her an air of maturity, even though she didn't have more than a few years on Naomi's own grand total of twenty-four.

Based on the woman's knowing glance, Naomi guessed that Mei had seen her gaping at Tomato-Shirt Guy. And Naomi had been gaping all right, no doubt about it.

But…well, Mei knew dang well that Naomi wasn't on the market. Back in Kane's Crossing, Naomi had gotten herself in such a tight spot with Bill Vassey that she had no business shopping around for another chance at failure here. Not for a while, at least.

Absently, she placed her hand over her tummy. More than two months along and counting. Naomi didn't know whether she was carrying a boy or a girl yet. She needed to get to the doctor for a second prenatal visit, and she would do it on the COBRAed health plan from her previous job—a plan she could barely afford. Heck, the vitamins she'd been advised to take by a friend from back home tested her slim budget enough already. Thank goodness the new job she'd gotten at Trinkets, a corporate chain of collectible shops, offered modest insurance for the future, so at least she was on her way.

Still, this child was hers—all hers. She was well into the best thing that'd ever happened to her, even if she'd needed to move away to start over with Baby.

It's all about you, sweetheart, and no one else. We're in this together.

As the soap came back on, everyone applauded, excited, and Naomi stood, intending to join the rest of the viewers who called themselves The Suds Club, named after the Laundromat itself.

Yet she never quite made it to her waiting seat in front of the TV.

Tomato-Shirt Guy was going at it with the dispenser again, fighting a lever. Sympathy fully evoked, Naomi held a finger up to Mei—*wait a sec*—then wandered toward him. The soft part of her just wanted to offer a little aid. She knew how much of a nightmare that machine could be. Also, in spite of her foster-care musical-chairs upbringing, she'd always been raised to be polite and helpful.

And being polite would hardly get her into trouble, would it?

By now, he'd regrouped, gotten out his wallet, and gone to the change machine, probably to replace the first batch of lost quarters. She knew the dispenser-eats-coin story all too well from her own initial visit.

His new position left her a view of his back. And what a back it was: broad, tapering into slim hips and a butt she'd—

Nope.

Back in possession of her common sense, she stood behind him and cleared her throat. But she wasn't prepared for the flare of heat that prickled her skin when he turned around.

Eyes so blue you couldn't *help* but gape.

For an endless second, Naomi couldn't form a single word. Not even a "hi." Not even the "yow" that struggled to escape her throat.

No, sir—instead she just stood there looking awkward, as country as corn bread next to a man who carried himself with such an obvious sense of self.

At least, that's what she thought until she realized that he was kind of gaping, too. He just wasn't doing it so blatantly. Instead, his gape was in his gaze—a flash of hesitation that she couldn't read worth anything.

Wait—maybe she'd just startled him. He'd been concentrating forcefully on his mission, after all; and here she was, sneaking up on him.

Quickly—or *efficiently* might've been the better description—he looked at her as a man might look at a maid who'd stumbled into his hotel room when he was least expecting it. Civil, but with a touch of "What can I help you with?" aloofness.

Naomi ignored a twinge of self-consciousness. Back home, her appearance had always been an issue: since her mother had given her up when she was tiny, Naomi didn't know where her own olive skin came from or what race she was. There was no doubt some mixed blood in her, but she couldn't exactly say from where.

"I—" She pointed back toward the detergent dispenser. "I noticed your…challenge…in engaging our raging soap monster. I've got a touch with that thing if you'd like me to give it a go for you."

He cocked a brow, suddenly all male pride. Impressive, how he could pull it off even while wearing a food-splattered shirt.

"Actually," he said, voice low and measured, "I think I can—" He cut himself off, his face going serious, as if a particularly vexing thought had entered his mind.

But then he exhaled, his features relaxing. Funny, though, how relaxing seemed to cause him some effort.

"You have a 'touch'?" he repeated.

Their gazes locked, and she told herself not to blush, don't blush, don't—

Abruptly, she turned away, skin burning. She focused on fishing a few quarters from her skirt pocket to prime the machine. Meanwhile, she keenly sensed him in back of her.

Heat, awareness.

She shook all that off by listening to *Flamingo Beach*. The main couple, Dash and Trina, traded star-crossed lover dialogue. But it sounded like gibberish right now, as untranslatable as the messages her brain was sending to her unsure fingers.

You're not on the market, she kept telling herself. *Not even remotely.*

While she fiddled with the dispenser, breathing in the powdered cleanliness of its detergents, she felt his eyes on her.

A delicious rush. Oooh, such a bad tingle.

She cleared her throat again, sneaking a peek behind her and smiling.

And—sure enough—he *was* watching.

Yes! Er…no. She didn't want him checking her out. Why complicate her life when that was the last thing she needed?

She swiveled back around to the dispenser, heart in her throat.

Not on the market….

The lever loosened up, just on the edge of giving in, and Naomi bolstered herself again before she beat the machine then had to turn around to see Tomato-Shirt Guy's blue, blue eyes. All she had to do was rest her hand over her belly—a connection, a real reason to stay strong.

One-handed, Naomi gradually persuaded that lever just a tad more, determined not to allow the pleasant shock of the stranger's blue eyes to rattle her once she finished.

After all there was Baby to consider.

And there was her own bruised heart and pride, too.

David Chandler wasn't used to having these kinds of days.

As he waited out the slender, friendly woman who'd

so easily approached him to offer help, he wondered if his mortification was obvious.

Him, the man who was so used to the well-greased flow of perfectly timed meetings that allowed him to acquire multimillion-dollar TV and radio stations, hotels and properties ripe for takeovers.

The CEO of a billion-dollar-plus empire.

"So," she said as she finessed the machine, her back still to him, "I'm guessing this is an unexpected laundry trip for you?"

"Right. My hotel's in the city and I wasn't about to go back there for another shirt." Plus, he didn't add, the idea of wearing a tomato stain the rest of the day, whether he was merely wandering the sidewalks of Placid Valley or not, was unthinkable. "I didn't come upon any clothes stores yet and I didn't know when I would. Then I saw the laundry."

Once more, his veins crackled with frozen frustration just at the thought of how he had lost control of his day so damned quickly.

Get it together.

And…there.

He never resorted to frustration. Never. And that's why most of The Chandler Corporation—or TCO— believed their CEO was made of unbreakable ice.

"Then welcome to The Suds Club," she said, tossing a smile back at him as she slowly worked the machine's lever. Her fingers were slim, feminine.

As she turned back around to finish her job, he said, "Glad to be here." Not that he really was, but running into a friendly local was at least a positive.

A very pretty local, too.

Maybe a less high-strung person would chat more with her, small talking and perhaps telling her all about how he'd come to have tomato on his chest, but that wasn't what David did. He was more used to commanding, and he wasn't sure he knew what to say to…well, a normal person. Someone he'd never related to very much as a perpetual boss.

Boss. His mind went into overdrive. How was everything running without him back in New York?

A weight seemed to press down on his chest, and he clamped off that line of useless thinking.

Even though this unease was dogging him more often than he liked, he had to trust that his older half brother, Lucas, was handling everything well back at TCO headquarters. He'd done it for a year and a half now, ever since stepping out of his former-playboy sandbox to assume his rightful place in running the family company.

Business associates, society, the press—all of them had been shocked at Lucas's turnaround, but David knew what had reformed the rake. Marriage. Marriage to a woman named Alicia. Somehow, she'd tamed the Don Juan and now he was the Happy Family Man and Business Success of the Decade.

The irony was that David had *manipulated* them into that marriage.

The weight pressed down on him even harder now. He wasn't proud of his part in the scheme, even though things had turned out for the best; the couple had fallen in love, in spite of all the lies David had encouraged Lucas to tell in order to win over an innocent, unknowing Alicia. She'd truly thought Lucas was in love with her, but he was actually using her good reputation for publicity.

When the couple had finally come to terms with what had happened, David couldn't bring himself to revel in their happy ending. His conscience wouldn't allow it. Nothing could excuse the coldness of his machinations.

More and more lately, he'd tried to block out his brother and his wife, but avoidance never seemed to work. It was even tougher now, when this very woman in front of him recalled Alicia at first glimpse. It was only after she'd started talking in her Southern-tinged drawl that David had snapped out of his surprise at the passing resemblance.

Like Lucas's wife, this woman had riotous curly brown hair, yet where Alicia's was longer and darker, this stranger wore hers in a chin-length bob. Also, her eyes were wider and smokier—an olive shade. Sweet-featured with generous lips, this woman was a little taller and slimmer, too, her skin duskier than Alicia's Latina complexion.

It wasn't that he had "feelings" for Alicia. Truthfully, David's interest had more to do with wanting what Lucas had; he was attracted to their *relationship*. And David was actually happy for his sibling—that wasn't an issue, either.

However, he *was* envious, and it shamed him.

At that, he found himself looking away from the woman and toward the crowd intently watching a soap opera. He drew back into his comfortable, cold shell again, his pulse resuming its rhythm, a beat he controlled. In the aftermath of meeting this woman—what had it been…an instant attraction?—he realized that their first moment of eye contact had acted like a shot of adrenaline to his system. It felt addictive, but wrong, too, because his interest in her was no doubt all about competing with his brother.

The weight was almost robbing him of breath by now.

David had to get rid of this envy that plagued him. Hell, that's why he had embarked upon this "vacation." Redemption. That's all he needed.

All he craved.

The woman's perky twang broke into him. "There! I think I've solved your soap problem. The machine should be all set up for you to make your choice."

At first, David reverted to his usual reactionary armor, arranging his features into an unreadable mask because he hadn't been able to manage the simple act of dealing with a dispenser himself. But then he wondered why his pride was necessary in a place where no one knew him or expected him to be the all-powerful boss of everything.

He concentrated on relaxing: first his shoulders, then the rest of him. He even offered a modest smile, and she returned it. The gesture speared him somewhere in his chest, in an area where he wasn't used to feeling.

"I appreciate your... 'touch.'"

The flow of his own tone surprised him. Somewhat pleased him, because he never thought relating could be this damned simple.

"Believe me," she said, laughing, probably because he was proving not to be some psycho who'd just wandered in to slay a detergent machine, "I had it out with this beast *my* first day here. But, somehow, I got the best of it. Which detergent are you after?"

"Any of them."

He motioned toward the machine, welcoming her to

take it on again. As she smiled and turned to the dispenser, the scent of her hair made him close his eyes for a long moment. Spearmint shampoo? he wondered. So soft, fresh.

Jokingly, she made a show of her magical "touch," wiggling her fingers. Then she gave the middle knob a good goose, jamming it downward until a tiny water-fall-decorated box popped out.

"My favorite brand." She held it out to him with a slightly proud grin. "It should be good for that stain you're wearing."

Her grin turned into a dazzling smile.

And there went David's chest again. Something throbbed there this time, as if tapping out a tangled signal, body to brain. He couldn't decipher it.

He accepted the detergent from her, then thought perhaps he should use his other hand to extend a greeting. "Thanks again. I'm Dav—" He stopped himself, deciding to shorten his given name for some reason…maybe because *David* sounded more impressive in a boardroom and didn't matter so much here. "Dave," he finished. "I'm Dave."

"Glad to meet you. I'm Naomi." She took his hand, soft skin sliding against his own rougher palm.

That was the end of David and the beginning of Dave—a fresh start for a person who sorely needed changing.

He held on to Naomi's hand, greeting her.

And hopefully greeting a new man in himself, as well.

Chapter Two

A buried warmth rose to the surface of his palm as he recognized how small her hand was in his. A spark traveled from his fingers, up his arm and down to his belly, where another, more dangerous clenching took root.

Speechless, he unclasped at the same moment she did. Her eyes had gone a little wider.

Was it his imagination or did she seem flustered?

Doubtful. David wasn't the type who made women's hearts go pitter-patter. That was Lucas's territory. David was more the quiet, behind-the-scenes guy who calculated every move then acted only if it would get him somewhere…even with women.

"Well, Dave," Naomi said, folding her arms in front of her chest, "you've got some work ahead of you."

Suddenly aware that there was something else besides

the two of them, he glanced down at his new, starched shirt, where a red stain blazed. He'd almost forgotten.

"This is what I got instead of lunch at that Italian place a few doors down," he said, the story coming more naturally now that he'd unclenched a little. *Dave, not David.* "Two kids tore out of the restaurant, but the second one had a tomato in his hand. He launched it at the boy he was chasing, but he missed." He thought for a second, then decided that Dave would add, "Lucky me."

"Oh, the Amati boys. They're handfuls. I can hear them playing—*yelling*—almost every day from inside my apartment." At his quizzical look, she added, "I live next door to the restaurant."

"Prime property, huh?"

"Well…" She shrugged, and it was sweet, cute. "Actually, my friend from high school's allowing me to crash at her place. Right now she's off on international flight duty as a 'glorified sky waitress.' Really, that's what she calls it."

David realized that he was having a *normal,* decent conversation with someone. Hell, if he were to take a step outside himself, he would even venture to say that he didn't resemble David Chandler, billionaire shark, at all. He liked the feeling.

But as he kept looking at himself from the outside, he knew that he hadn't changed much. Sure, instead of a designer suit, he was wearing a new "casual" wardrobe he'd purchased at Nordstrom this morning. He was in denim rather than silk, but what was the difference, really? He was still the same stiff.

Near the television, a few women oohed at something on the screen.

Then an odd notion occurred to him: if he sat down with those normal, middle-class people, could he convince them that he was one of them?

The mere possibility lightened the pressure that constantly haunted him. What if he could…?

No, he wouldn't even think of it. The weight pressed down full force again.

At the oohs, Naomi had spun around to catch what was happening on the TV, too. Someone named Delia had broken into Trina and Dash's romantic reunion. He had no idea who Trina and Dash were, but they seemed very important.

"That's no good," Naomi said, turning back toward him. Then she shook her head, as if to leave Trina and Dash behind. Her gaze came to land on his shirt again, and she looked thoughtful. "Say…I've got a stain remover that might work even better than detergent. I should've thought of that before." She bopped herself in the head with a splayed hand. "I'm the sloppiest eater ever, and I carry this stuff at all times…."

She dug into a purse that was slung crosswise over her chest. The bag's bulkiness covered most of her long, faded, flowered sundress. After she pulled a small can out of her bag, she gave it to him.

"Here. This is a miracle. It's trampled the ketchup out of my clothes before."

David automatically reached for his wallet. "I appreciate it. How much…?"

"Oh, no. It's yours. I've got another can at my place."

That's when it hit him—these people didn't expect to be compensated for everything, whether payment

came in cash or future favors. He reveled in the anonymity for a moment.

If they knew who he really was—and how much he
was worth—would they be so welcoming and casual?
The thought was sobering.

"Thanks," he said simply.

It was enough to bring out another smile from Naomi.
A pause lingered, an awkward moment between two
strangers not knowing what else to say to each other.

"Well…" David gestured toward a washer.

"All right." Naomi raised a hand in farewell, then
backed toward the TV crowd. "Good luck with that."

As she departed, David attempted to put Naomi aside
and make sense out of the stain remover. He read the directions and realized that his shirt would have to basically
marinate in the spray before he could do anything else with
it. Who knew? He had a maid who collected his laundry
every day and what happened from there was a mystery.

Not that he couldn't figure this out.

He took off his button-down, noticing that his undershirt was also blushed with tomato. Damn it, he didn't
want to be "that guy" who ran around a laundry shirt-
less. Didn't stuff like that just happen in TV ads anyway?

In the end, he decided he would spray Naomi's wonder
stuff on the undershirt while he wore it. Or would that be
worse than hanging out in his skin like Wonderstud?

Out of pure instinct, he glanced up to find Naomi
watching him. There was a soft, wondering gleam in her
eyes, but she looked away so quickly that he would
never have called her on it. But he could call *himself* on
the electricity suddenly zinging over his skin.

He couldn't help but withdraw into himself again, so

he was taken aback when an Asian woman with long hair approached him with a black shirt.

"I thought this might be about your size. My... husband's got a similar build."

She quickly left, exchanging a cryptically wounded glance with Naomi, who stood in the back of the viewing chairs as if reluctant to commit to sitting.

Then Naomi sent David a friendly grin, erasing the strained moment.

He held up the shirt, addressing the other woman's retreating back. "I'll return this to you soon."

The lady merely nodded back at him, raising her hand in acknowledgment. She sat and resumed folding clothes from one chair to the other.

For a moment, a flash of thought caused him to wonder what the woman expected from him in return, and shame choked him. Since he wasn't as warm or giving as other people, he didn't understand why *they* acted so naturally and *he* didn't.

Well, he was trying to make himself understand. To find the human heart inside the corporate raider.

A blonde resembling a Hitchcock heroine got out of her own chair, almost inconspicuously enough to make David believe she wasn't checking him out. He immediately recognized her as a fellow corporate animal: she had the collected energy of one.

As she headed toward the soda machine in the rear of the room, she passed someone tucked into a corner while tapping away on a laptop computer. Much to David's surprise, he saw that it was a man garbed in who-cares-how-old-these-are blue jeans and a loose, long-sleeved white shirt that barely covered a thin T-shirt. Dark-brown hair and a goatee completed his ensemble.

On the blonde's way back, the man flashed a devilish smile at her—one that she expertly ignored while taking a delicate swig from her beverage.

The man merely shook his head and chuckled, keeping an eye on the TV.

David almost laughed out loud. A reluctant male soap fan? It could be true, judging from the way the guy was trying so hard to disguise his interest in the show.

The discovery prompted David to look at the others—*really* look since he rarely took the time to notice personal things unless it would benefit him. He saw a vibrant Indian woman wearing a sheer orange wrap over her long printed skirts, a spike-haired redhead with punky boots giggling at something a soap character just said, a brunette garbed in bike-riding gear…

Then his attention settled on Naomi, who turned back to the TV as if she hadn't been measuring him, too.

His body responded with such power he wondered if he'd ever really felt an attraction for anyone before. There'd been lust, that was for certain, but this was different—a twisting, sharp longing, an out-of-control urge that pinned him in place.

But he was feeling it for all the wrong reasons, wasn't he? She reminded him of what his dad was always riding him about.

When are you going to find a true woman like Lucas did, David?

He shut himself down, suspecting that he was incapable of this one thing in life: one thing that Lucas the former screwup had triumphed in while David the former golden boy had failed.

With too much force, David shucked off his undershirt, pressed it over a washing machine's lid, then yanked the black T-shirt over his head. Testing the snug fit, he glanced down at himself, only to notice the small logo in the right corner of the front pocket. A hand flying the middle finger.

From near the chairs, he heard a stifled laugh.

It was Naomi. She shrugged, gave one last glimpse to the TV and wandered over. "I'm sorry. It's just that you don't seem the type to be so…expressive. Mei's husband…ex-husband…whatever he is…can be a tad…"

She waved her hands around.

"Rebellious?" He sprayed both of his shirts with the stain remover, then held the can up to Naomi again.

"No, really," she said. "Keep it. You never know when the Amati kids are going to tag you."

"I probably won't be around long enough for that to happen."

She paused, then nodded, looking a little out of place. It tugged at David's chest.

"You're just passing through town?" she asked.

"Yes." How much should he tell her? He decided to stretch the truth, just in case his infatuation with not being David Chandler wore off—just in case he failed in the attempt. If so, he'd be gone before the press ever got wind that he'd been here anyway, and these people would never know who they'd been talking to. Being a Chandler invited the cameras, even though he'd never reached Lucas-like proportions, where the paparazzi trailed him everywhere. "I walked around the city yesterday," he added, "then here in Placid Valley today, but I thought I'd hit wine country tomorrow."

"Oh, you're on vacation?"

He nodded. A vacation from himself.

"From where?" she added.

"Manhattan."

"I knew it—a big-city boy. I wish I'd lived here longer because I'd suggest a good winery or something. Not that I do much drinking."

Here, she looked out of sorts again, lowering her head and plucking at her prim sundress. She looked pretty in the simple design.

As if to wipe away the thought, he found himself talking again. "How long have you lived here?"

"About two weeks."

"Let me guess." He risked a smile. It felt right, so he kept it, especially since she responded with one of her own—one that warmed him from head to toe. "You're from the South."

"Right, but you can be more specific than that." She leaned her hip against a machine, narrowing her eyes. "*Where* in the South?"

David had done extensive traveling, but mainly to cosmopolitan areas where business demanded it. He racked his brain anyway. "Tennessee."

"Think more north."

He kicked into assessment mode, his brain going visual, just as it did when he needed to pull up information in a meeting. A map superimposed itself over his gaze, and he quickly made another choice. "Kentucky."

"Bingo! Two guesses. Not bad for a big-city boy."

Her enthusiasm was almost contagious. "You miss it there?"

"Me? I don't…" She pursed her lips. "Sometimes, I guess I do."

Her answer was so curious that he was intrigued. There was genuine melancholy there. Why?

Just then, his cell phone rang and, when he checked the ID screen, he saw Lucas's home number. He had to take this, mostly because, at this time of day, his brother was at the office and that meant someone else might be calling.

He told Naomi that he would be back and moved toward the exit. He meant it, too. He would come back because, oddly, being around her seemed to make him feel less…burdened.

Now he just had to figure out how to feel that way all the time.

As he emerged outside, the early-September air had a light bounce to it. Strange—before he'd gone inside the Laundromat, it'd smelled like an average stale town bordering a big city. But now there was a trace of garlic on the breeze, the lace of salt from the nearby bay and a sweet wash of flowers from a window box attached to a boutique's facade.

He answered the phone to hear his four-year-old nephew say, "Uncle!"

Gabriel was one of two people who could make him smile anywhere and everywhere; his one-year-old niece Phoebe was the other.

"You sneaking on the phone to call me again?" David asked playfully, knowing how Gabe loved to escape his mom and make random calls to David at the office while she took care of him at the penthouse.

"Mama let me. Where are you?"

Since David had left a few days ago, everyone from Lucas to his dad had been calling to ask this same question. He'd returned the calls to let them know he was fine, of course, but he kept his whereabouts close to his chest for now. And even though he wanted to tell Gabe, he wouldn't. He needed to feel lost.

"I'm someplace safe and warm," he answered. "I'm all right, but I miss you a lot."

"I miss you, too."

David fisted his hand before that place in his chest could constrict first.

"When're you coming back?" Gabe added.

"Soon. And I'll bring you and Phoebe some treats. How does that sound?"

"Tweats!" the boy said. He'd developed trouble with his Rs. David secretly loved that, even though he kept it to himself.

"Then it's a deal." David turned toward the Laundro-mat door when it opened. One of the soap watchers, the Asian woman, walked out, nodding at him as she detoured into a market a few yards down.

He blew out a breath, and realized he was relieved that it hadn't been Naomi leaving.

Shaking his head, he told himself to cut it out, then went back to talking with his nephew.

To one of the only soft spots David had ever allowed himself.

After Mei left to pick up an after-school snack for her four-year-old daughter, Naomi kept her eye on the door. It hadn't been the first time she'd looked over there since David had walked out, either. And every instant she found herself waiting for him to come back in, she chided herself.

Aren't you the girl who's trying to get away from men? she asked herself. *Isn't it sort of a bad idea to entertain the notion of getting involved with someone else?*

Not that she was "getting involved" here. A few sparking glances between her and the stranger and Naomi thought it was love. Hah. Far from it. But there was definite chemistry, at least on her side, and it concerned her.

Just keep your mind on the wash and your future, she thought. *You can't handle anything else right now.*

While eyeing the TV, she piled her whites in the basket she'd borrowed from the apartment. Carissa, her barely there roommate, used it when she was in town to do laundry at night.

"I see what's going down," said a voice next to her. Jenny.

"Just daydreaming," Naomi said.

The blonde made a yeah-right face. "Just admit to some good, grade-A quality, innocent flirting, Naomi."

"Flirting?" Who, her?

"Flirting. You had that body language, leaning toward him, smiling, blushing. Hi, that's flirting."

"I don't have the luxury of doing that." Naomi pulled her basket toward her. "I—"

"It's that creep back home who got you pregnant." Jenny had lowered her voice. Even so, Liam McCree peered up from his computer near the back of the room. Naomi had forgotten he was even there, which was strange. Usually he heckled and poked fun at the soap opera. Maybe he was on a Web-site-designing deadline today or something.

"Okay, you're right," Naomi said softly. "But that doesn't mean I need to run right out and get another boyfriend to take his place. I don't need a husband or a caretaker."

Jenny widened her deep blue eyes at Naomi's strident tone. "So keep it light. Have some fun."

That's right—unlike Naomi and even Mei, who was having marital difficulties with her firefighting husband, Jenny was a so-called serial dater. Every Wednesday, she came to the Club armed with tales of weekend dates that never seemed to pan out. But that didn't keep her from trying.

"And above all," Jenny added, "keep being kind to anyone who happens in here with tomato all over his button-down."

"That, my friend, is what I was being—kind. It had nothing to do with flirting."

"Well, then, maybe you might consider going a step further. There's that vintage store, right down the street, that he could benefit from. I'd show him there, myself, but work is calling me back to my place. Lunch hour can't last forever, even if I am on my own schedule today."

"Jenny…"

"I'm just saying that you could flirt…er…*kind* your way down the street and get him settled at Bowler's. That's as far as your new friendship would have to go."

Naomi opened her mouth to retort, but the other woman merely tilted her head.

"Kindness, Naomi. The man's wearing a shirt with an R-rated logo."

The flying finger. Ugh.

At that, Naomi's better instincts took over: the friendly small-town girl who would go out of her way to lend a hand if people would just allow her the opportunity.

So...the vintage store. Dave was in need of something decent to wear. Why not just point him to the shop and that would be that? A good turn from a good girl. That's all....

The bell on the Laundromat door dinged, and Naomi turned to find Dave entering, that silly T-shirt clinging to his wide chest as he tucked his phone into a pocket. Oxygen deserted her. He was smiling, emotion suffusing his eyes with a liveliness Naomi hadn't noticed before; it transformed him from mere handsome babe into knee-gelling god.

Help him out, take him to the shop. No expectations. And maybe he'll even remind you that good guys exist.

Dave came closer, and Naomi took a deep breath, then let it out.

"Dave?" she ventured.

When he transferred his smile to her, her heart expanded.

"How about ditching Mei's husband's shirt for something more dignified at the vintage store down the block?" she asked.

She felt her knees go wobbly.

"Good store," Jenny said from her side of the Laundromat. "Big selection."

Then the next part rushed right out before Naomi could stop it. "I'll show you the way. What do you say?"

Chapter Three

Had Naomi just asked him out?

David turned the possibility over in his mind, only to conclude that he was misinterpreting her intentions. She was merely doing him another favor. It'd started with the spray cleaner, then continued with Mei lending a shirt.

And now this group of strangers was offering to make sure he didn't look like a middle-finger-flipping-T-shirt-wearing fool around town.

He came to a stop near a high folding table, then rested an arm on it. The position made his upscale "casual" clothes feel even stiffer, as if they were foreign to him. In fact, they felt just as confining as a business suit.

What if he could get some worked-in jeans from this store they were talking about? Would it complete Dave, the man who was becoming more and more comfortable around here by the second?

"Not that I don't appreciate this shirt," he said, "but I wouldn't say no to shopping around for another look."

Naomi widened her eyes, as if surprised at his acceptance, and motioned toward the door, clutching her purse strap over her chest as she strolled toward it.

While catching up, he couldn't help watching Naomi's swaying hips. She was slender, but it seemed that most of her was concentrated in her derriere. He was so used to the New York fashion set and their clothes-hanger figures that seeing some actual curves sent a twang through him, making him all but vibrate during their short walk past a candy shop, a market then a plant boutique.

When they got to Bowler's, the vintage shop, the *bing* of an electric bell welcomed them inside. The slight scent of old clothes and dry-cleaning must hovered while a Frank Sinatra standard played. A woman wearing dark cat-eye glasses waved at them from the rack of furry coats she was organizing. They said hi back, then Naomi headed straight for the men's section against a far wall.

"I see the pièce de résistance already," she said, pulling a loud Hawaiian shirt out of a colorful clutter.

She laughed even before David's eyes got the full blast of flowery patterns. This close, he noticed that she had a slight dimple in her chin. It melted something inside of him.

"On second thought, I'm not sure you're the type to travel the tiki route." She moved to another rack and sifted through the material.

"What's my type then?"

The question echoed in his mind, and he held his

breath. What was his type? God, he hoped she wouldn't say, "Something with the personality of a board. A real snooze. Booo-ring."

Instead, she assessed him, narrowing her olive-hued eyes.

"If I were to guess, I'd venture that you're…" Naomi hesitated, looking him up and down.

At the brush of her gaze, David's flesh seemed to shift, as if madly trying to become a part of a different person. The muscles of his belly flexed as he took the opportunity to slowly peruse her, also, while she wasn't noticing.

Her hair—it was all wild curls, sexy and free. And that skin—it'd be so smooth if he touched her cheek, ran a thumb over her palm…

Uninvited, the image of him clasping her hand and bringing her into a room where he would introduce her to his father sneaked into David's brain.

See, he would say, *Now I'm as good as my brother. Are you happy?*

Are you happy…?

Naomi had finished her analysis of him and, seeming satisfied with what she'd found, had already chosen another shirt. When he finally tore his gaze away from her to inspect it, David couldn't help a laugh.

"That's the type of guy you think I am?" he asked.

She was holding out a plain burgundy T-shirt, stark in its cotton blandness.

Naomi apparently caught his puzzlement, taking a second look at the material on its hanger, then another glance back at him.

"*Guys* wear shirts without cute slogans or advertisements. Real guys—men." She blushed for some reason. "Or would you rather go back to the luau nightmare?"

"No, but... Isn't it kind of plain?" So unlike his regular designer suits.

But wasn't that the point?

Wait, maybe he was missing the point altogether. Shouldn't he be ecstatic that she'd picked a "man" shirt? Didn't that mean she saw past his new, starched jeans and into what he really wanted to be—a guy people didn't shrink back from when he entered a room because his tough reputation preceded him?

Knowing that her choice had actually been a compliment, he gently took the shirt from her. "You're right. This is more me."

Naomi folded her arms over her chest again, seemingly bashful since their errand had been completed. But the planklike quality of his denims was nagging at him now.

"How about...?" He gestured to his jeans. "And a few more shirts. My trip was sudden and I didn't pack very well."

The thought of going back to his fancy hotel and tossing out his starchy clothes for some old ones with personality gave him a sense of possible liberty.

But David didn't stop there. Hell, why not check out of that hotel in favor of something more modest? A place where he could abandon all pretense?

And, just like that, he could breathe, maybe even for the first time in his life.

As Naomi threw herself into finding more plain shirts, she asked, "Why was your trip sudden? If you don't mind me asking."

"It was one of those things where I just needed to get away."

There—not a lie, exactly, but it wasn't forthcoming. He wasn't about to tell her who he really was and, besides, he didn't want to think about what his father had said to him—then what had happened in the office a few days ago—to jump-start this trip across the country. It would take away everything he'd just found in the Laundromat—a hidden corner of the world that he'd never suspected existed.

"Understood." Her face seemed to reflect a certain disappointment in his vagueness. But when she raised another shirt to him, it covered her expression. "How's this?"

A navy-blue color this time. "Good. Listen, Naomi, I don't mean to sound evasive, but…"

"Oh, no. Don't apologize for my nosiness." She laid the shirt over her arm, then began searching for another. "I shouldn't be in your personal business." She sighed. "Something I need to improve on, I guess."

Absently, she tugged at the material of her dress over her stomach, a casual reaction. But when she snatched her hand away, as if correcting a bad habit, David wondered why it seemed symbolic of something more.

She wandered to a rack littered with threadbare jeans, clearly trying to avoid him.

For once, David allowed himself to say what was actually on his mind: no manipulative demeanor, no careful words. "I don't think you need to worry much about improving yourself, Naomi."

As soon as the naked compliment hit the air, his skin heated. Voicing his emotions was startling; it made him feel relatively bare, as if revealing something more under his flesh. But was that true? Was there a better, warmer being under there somewhere?

Was there hope for getting what Lucas had, after all?

It felt odd to be so honest with another person. No, actually, it was terrifying.

Out of pure instinct, he raised his ice shields again, forcing his face into a study of collected cool as she turned to face him.

She looked…a little sad. "I wish I didn't need improvement. I really do."

A switch flipped on inside David, a mechanism wired by curiosity. What made her think that way? What had darkened her eyes at his comment?

A woman of substance and complexity, that's what you need. David could almost hear his dad saying it. *Lucas found someone like that—you should be able to, also.*

Once again, envy ate at David, but he fought it. His brother *deserved* happiness—but maybe David didn't.

Out of the depths of a rack, Naomi pulled out a puke-green shirt and gave him a cheeky, questioning glance.

They both cracked up, knowing she was joking. It was much easier to concentrate on baroque vomit-hued shirts than the thread of awareness connecting *them.*

Ignoring the sparks, David went about going into the dressing room, keeping the burgundy T and a pair of jeans on, then purchasing everything in one fell swoop. He noticed that Naomi hadn't chosen a single item for herself.

When he said something about it, she answered, "I'm good for clothes." She brushed a hand over her long sundress.

He took a good look at her wardrobe, noting the

slightly faded colors surrounding the flowered pattern. Maybe she was on a budget?

"Hey, listen, pick anything you want, and—"

"No, really." She'd gotten serious. "I'm good, Dave."

As he settled the bill, he realized his error on a couple of levels. He'd obviously taken a swipe at her pride. Also, a regular guy wouldn't be running around telling people to engage in shopping sprees while he footed the bill.

The inability to show his appreciation by lavishing gifts unsettled him. How else could he say thank you for her time? Damn, he wasn't good at this type of thing.

He tried the most obvious method as they walked out of the store. "I'm sure you had a million other things to be doing, so…thanks, Naomi. You really helped."

Not in all the years he'd bought diamonds and flowers for women had he seen one light up in this way. Naomi's smoky eyes sparkled, and her smile made the afternoon sun seem dim. He got wary of what might happen next.

"I was glad to do it." She glanced away, at the ground, changing the tone of their conversation. "Had to save you from public indecency, you know."

She started laughing, and the sound of it jiggered something within David. It cut loose a wish that'd been building inside of him for the last hour or so. It shaped his desire into one word.

"Coffee," he said.

That's right—just one inarticulate word that he couldn't take back, even though he knew he was asking her to be with him a little longer for all the wrong reasons: competition with his brother, pleasing his father.

But David realized something else. He felt different

around this woman. In fact, a hollowness inside him had actually stopped echoing this last half hour while he'd been around her.

Fulfillment?

The word sped through his consciousness before he could ignore it.

No. It was too strong a description for what he was trying to figure out right now.

Wasn't it?

At Naomi's confused look, he forged on, hardly believing he had it in him to be this awkward. Calling up Dave's easiness, he did his best to save himself.

"How about some coffee before you go out to save another poor tomato-target like me?"

She bit her lip, as if not knowing how to answer. Great. Maybe he'd also misinterpreted her kindness. Maybe he didn't know how to deal with people outside of his own warped bubble of existence….

"If you can't—" he began.

"I'm just thinking of when I have to go into work. Two-thirty. That's when my shift starts at Trinkets." She swallowed hard as she gestured down the street. "It's this collectible shop in the mall…."

"I know it." Holy crap, his company *owned* that chain. TCO had recently acquired its mother corporation.

"But, I think I can swing an hour for amusement," she added. "Can I just drop my laundry off at my place? There's actually a coffee nook just past our vintage store."

Our vintage store. Good God, they were already into joint property. The stupid thought made David's pulse skyrocket.

She must've taken his silence—his "duh, what do I

do now?" pause—for a go, because she grinned and darted ahead to the Laundromat. "See you there in fifteen, okay?"

Not knowing what else to do, he raised a hand in acquiescence, watching as she disappeared into the Laundromat.

If the possibility of what lay ahead hadn't already given him so much hope, David would've squashed this deal right then and there.

Shortly thereafter, Naomi rushed out of her apartment building's exit and onto the sidewalk, barely able to keep her heart in her chest.

What had happened? The day had started out fine, with her doing laundry, and then it'd gone all *Alice in Wonderland*. She was going out to "coffee" with a man.

Bad idea, bad idea. The words echoed every footstep she took toward the coffee shop, yet what was the big deal? It wasn't as if she was getting engaged to Dave...yeesh, what was his last name? See, this wasn't even a real date—the man didn't even possess a last name! So why was she getting all nervous?

She passed the Laundromat, peeking inside. None of The Club remained—they'd all left while she was at the vintage store with Dave. So Naomi had headed to her own apartment, bursting with her Dave coffee news, but not knowing who to tell about it. There wasn't time for that anyway.

Besides, she reminded herself, *you are transitioning here. No romance allowed.*

That's because back in Kane's Crossing she'd been so taken in by a guy's charm that she'd temporarily lost her mind and told herself she'd felt enough affection for him to go all the way. Even worse, she'd pretty much been ditched by her baby's dad when he'd gone out of town on a long sales trip.

Stupid, *stupid* her. All her life, she'd been naive about men. Not enough to get into situations like this exactly, but she'd always been too trusting. That wasn't to say she'd slept around though—oh, no, when a girl grew up with not much more than her first name, pride was as good as gold—but she had possessed a pretty wild reputation in high school. Hanging out with the smokers in the lunch court seemed to encourage that, but in reality, she wasn't *too* bad.

Well, maybe a little, but not that much.

After graduating, she'd actually tried to clean up her image, taking more care with her clothes and toning down the makeup. She'd also attempted to keep her eyes wide-open with men, learning date by date who was the right kind of guy and who was wrong. But when Bill Vassey came to town, he'd been so sincere and impressive, with his sales rep job for a restaurant supply company and all his convincing ambitions. She'd actually been so besotted that she hadn't even *thought* he wouldn't want a family with her when it came right down to it, even if he had told her differently.

Unfortunately, she'd been dumb enough to think that when faced with their pregnancy from a broken condom he would love her enough to change his mind.

Yes, having the family she'd always wanted—even by accident—had been an innocently premature expectation with Bill. Still, the last thing she'd expected him to do was act shocked, then blurt out that they should think about terminating her pregnancy.

That's what she got for surprising him with the news just as he was leaving late for the airport, she supposed.

"We'll talk later," he'd said, checking his watch and shooting her a look that pleaded for understanding. "We'll have a long, long talk, all right? This is something to really sit down over, not settle right now or even on the phone. Okay, Naomi? Just wait for me to get back and we'll deal with everything."

The shock of it had finally flicked her brain on. That night, she'd taken a look around the conservative small town where she'd been raised in foster home after foster home, realizing that if she stayed here caring for a child all on her own, her baby would be labeled just like Naomi. *Trash. Bastard.*

Naomi wouldn't stand for any of that name-calling. Why put her child in that kind of situation when it was avoidable? And since Bill obviously didn't want either of them all that much, why not cut the few ties she had and start fresh somewhere new?

It wasn't as if her job ringing up customers at the grocery was enough to keep her in Kane's Crossing. And it wasn't as if she had family there, either. So she'd called Carissa, who'd escaped Kane's Crossing long ago to become a flight attendant. She was based in San Francisco and, miracle of miracles, she'd said it'd be great to see Naomi again. And would she consider apartment-sitting while Carissa was off flying the blue skies?

Naomi accepted right away, promising herself that she would do everything in her power to pay her friend back and that she wouldn't stay long—just enough to get on her feet and make a good life for her child. True, the San Fran area wasn't exactly the cheapest, but she'd be living rent-free. Plus, she was going to get a better job after taking classes at the community college, maybe even something that had to do with numbers. She'd always been great at math, even though she'd been iffy in most other subjects.

After taking care of all that, she'd phoned Bill, who was staying in a Cincinnati hotel room, and announced that she was leaving. But she wasn't sure he understood. Actually, he'd merely repeated that they'd talk about "all this" when he got back.

Now, after entering the coffee shop and spying Dave sitting at a far table as he scanned a newspaper, she forgot about her defenses. All she remembered was that, with this man, she didn't feel so much like trash anymore; he didn't know what they called her back home, and he didn't need to.

She approached the table, where he had laid his two shirts out on the chairs next to him, and he glanced up. For a bare second, she thought she saw something flash in his gaze—an emotion both exciting and scary—but then he got to his feet, his smile consuming her attention instead.

Yow.

A smile from him. He hadn't given out very many of those, but that was probably a good thing, because his smiles were likely to make her change her own mind.

Her heartbeat flared, then throbbed into a quick, tapping dance. She shouldn't be this happy to see him. It didn't make sense.

"Have any favorites on the menu?" he asked, his voice cracking a bit.

She took note of how his forehead furrowed as he cleared his throat. He seemed almost tentative around her now. Was he…?

Nah. She wouldn't even start to think he was attracted to her beyond saying thank you with some coffee.

"Apple juice," she said, thinking of Baby and how caffeine would be unhealthy for him or her.

A slow grin spread over his lips, and Naomi sat down before she fell down.

"Got it," he said, going to the counter and ordering.

It took every ounce of self-control not to check him out as she waited. Instead, she aimlessly peered around the room, trying to seem incredibly interested in the dark-wooded decor, the coffee-bean murals on the ceiling, the afternoon hush of people who were just here to hang out while reading. She noticed the stain remover was working well on his shirts and reminded herself to tell him he might want to apply another coating soon.

He was back before she'd gotten herself together— not that she was sure she could ever accomplish such a feat. Not with him around.

As he handed her a chilled bottle of apple juice, she glanced at his dark coffee.

"I like mine strong," he said. "Half the time, a wicked brew is all that keeps me going in life."

Again, she wondered what exactly it was that he did, why he'd failed to pack properly for a vacation. But it would be rude to pursue the subject, seeing as he'd pretty much shut down any explanation back at the vintage store.

"Coffee's never been my thing," she offered. Wow, how lame was this palaver?

He seemed to realize it, too, shooting her a knowing grin and leaning back in his chair. He was far more relaxed than earlier, when he'd first lorded it into The Suds Club to tangle with the detergent machine. Now, his body didn't seem to be carrying the same burden, and he appeared more open. She wished she knew what'd been bugging him earlier, but again—none of her business.

Except…heck, with the way he was affecting her, it sure was her business. His suddenly easy, frank way of sitting there was flustering her.

She took a sip of juice, stalling, not knowing what to say next.

He leaned on the table almost stiffly, almost as if too aware that he'd been smiling and he was now thinking better of it. But, then, he seemed to think about what he was doing *now,* and he reclined in his chair, resting an arm on the back of a second one. She was sure he meant to relax.

So why did it appear as if he'd also had to think about managing that?

"I noticed all your friends watching that soap opera in the laundry," he said. "Is it some sort of daily get-together?"

Neutral ground. She could swing with that. "Uh-huh, but usually there's more of a crowd. We're into *Flamingo Beach,* and I'm new to The Club, of course, having just moved here and all."

"Good way of making friends."

"I suppose that's how the best of friendships start, with people willing to step outside their normal comfort zones. A couple of the girls just came right on over to me and scooped me into their little group. Thank goodness someone else besides me took the first step because…heck, you know how it is in a new place, right? It's frightening trying to meet people."

"Right." He looked thoughtful, cupping his hands around his coffee mug. "Scary as hell."

They paused, both taking a drink as strains of classical music softly sang.

"Then…this *Flamingo Beach,*" Dave said. "I've never watched a soap opera. What's the draw?"

It was as if a fire had been lit under Naomi's butt. She sat up straight in her chair, saying grace to whatever had given him the urge to make this the subject of his small talk. She could talk about *FB* for days.

"You've never watched? My, do you have something to catch up on. I defy you to take in a week's worth of episodes, then see if you can wean yourself off of it. You kind of live through the characters, I guess. They endure all these highs and lows and you just ache for them when something goes wrong…."

She stopped because Dave looked so amused.

"What?" she asked.

"I don't know, it's…cute that you'd get so into it."

"Cute?" Naomi chuffed. "Was it cute when the bad girl, Delia, slipped something into Dash's drink and tried to make him think he'd betrayed Trina with her? I hardly think so."

Dave was by now shaking his head, as if watching a tennis match where the balls were the characters' names.

Naomi gave up, knowing this was a lost cause with any guy but Liam McCree, who would never admit to watching while "working" on his laptop.

"Maybe," he said, "I'll have to give it a go."

For a second, Naomi couldn't process. Had he just said...?

"Are you talking about *Flamingo Beach?*" she asked, testing.

He slipped his hands to the back of his head, elbows out as he fixed his gaze on the ceiling, smiling. The muscles in his arms strained, and she swallowed heavily.

"Why not?" he asked. "I didn't leave New York to keep myself from experiencing new things."

"Okay." Naomi leaned forward, snagging his attention again. He grinned and her skin went hot. "I'll even catch you up on the details if you really want to get into it."

"Sounds like a plan."

"We start tomorrow then, and after that you can go to the wine country."

"Tomorrow it is."

They locked stares, as if in some dare. Well, seeing as a lot of men looked upon soap-opera watching as a girlie thing, Naomi could see why this was an experience for Dave.

But when their stare steamed up, turning into something she was altogether unprepared for, Naomi's heart seemed to stop.

Not this, she thought. *Not anything beyond casual coffee and conversation....*

Her nerves got the best of her.

"I'm pregnant," she blurted, apropos of nothing except the fears running through her head. It was meant to discourage and nothing else.

Dave froze, clearly taken unawares. Then slowly, ever so slowly, he brought his arms down from his head. Back to the stiff man who'd walked into the Laundromat earlier today. Back to a place where Naomi could be more comfortable, with him as good as ten feet away from her.

"I see," he said.

The utter stupidity of her timing made her wish a meteor would hit the building right about now. Obliteration would feel better than this.

Knowing there was no other way around the tension, she charged ahead. "I just want to make things clear because we're having coffee. Not that 'coffee' means a whole lot but…" She sighed. "I just want to make things clear."

Oh, my God, could she be any more presumptuous? With every syllable she was going too far.

"Right now, the clarity's at about mud level." His stiffness had given way to wariness. He reminded her of an animal that wasn't sure whether you were about to pull out a gun or desert the area altogether. "Are you going to tell me about your husband or your boyfriend now…?"

"Neither," Naomi said softly. "I don't have either one of those."

It looked as though he wanted to ask more but didn't want to ask more at the same time, so Naomi spared him by talking. Not that she knew what was coming out of her mouth.

"I just want…" What? She had no idea.

But she knew the truth. Deep inside, she was wondering if the pregnancy news would put him across a canyon. That way, she could still depend on only herself and protect her baby from anyone who got too close before they could do them any harm.

Dave was still gauging her. "You just want…*coffee.*" The word held more significance than was obvious.

"Right, Naomi? Just…coffee with someone else who's new in town."

It made sense. *Coffee* didn't carry any expectation with it. *Coffee* was something you could forget after you went home to sleep at night without any worry of a promise made.

Relieved that he seemed to understand, Naomi raised her bottled juice to him, hoping for a truce. When he raised his own mug, she smiled, glad she'd made herself clear…as mud.

"To coffee then," she said as they clinked mugs. "Or even juice."

While she drank, she thought she heard her conscience give its own two cents.

Coffee, your foot, it said, making Naomi almost sputter out her beverage.

But, from that point on, her misgivings stayed dormant, thank goodness.

If only the same could be said about Naomi's ever-growing attraction to Dave.

Chapter Four

The next day, David made sure he arrived at The Suds Club just shy of noon, before the start of that soap opera.

But as he was walking toward the Laundromat, he found himself passing the entrance, ducking into the market next door instead.

There, he stood by a display of apples, hands on hips and reconsidering what the hell he was doing.

A pregnant woman, he thought. Whether he admitted it or not, he was kind-of-sort-of courting a girl with a sweet smile and a history that she hadn't elaborated on past the pregnancy bombshell.

So why was he doing it?

David knew only too well, because he could still hear the last thing Ford Chandler had said to him before David had taken off across the country.

"It's really a shame."

The old man had been watching Lucas with Alicia as they played with their adopted son, Gabriel, and their infant daughter, Phoebe, in front of the fireplace last Sunday evening.

David knew what was coming next, because he'd thought the same thing himself too many times to count.

"Shame that you haven't learned what Lucas did," good old dad continued, leaning on his cane, his lips tilted from a stroke that still slowed him down. He pointed a withered finger at Lucas, who was rough-housing with Gabe and causing the child to giggle. "There's a man who's not going to end up like his father. He won't regret anything when he's at the end of *his* road."

"Unlike me," David had said tightly.

Ford had turned to him, his eyes shaded. "You see how happy he is. You could have the same joy, David, if you'd look up from your contracts long enough to care. And you know I'm right—a man who's been divorced four times could be called an expert. Is this what you want for yourself?" The patriarch had gestured to his broken body. "You want to become *this?*"

This. What exactly was *this?* David wondered now. Was it a thirty-year-old man who had studied *The Art of War* and applied it to business practices? Was it a man who'd tested even his own ethical limits in the past?

Though David oftentimes watched Lucas and Alicia with a twinge of unidentifiable longing, he'd never con-sciously made plans to change. Not until after he'd gone home that same night to meet a woman. Afterward, she'd thanked him for the good time, and David knew he would never see her again. Women only called when they wanted a liaison that wouldn't be hard to get out of when they were satisfied. Up until now, David hadn't minded much—work was his priority, and a relationship would only drag him down.

But *everything* seemed to be giving voice to all his niggling doubts, and it was driving him to distraction.

The next day, he'd been so preoccupied with his last date, plus all of his father's blunt opinions, that he'd lost his edge in a meeting. It'd cost TCO at least a million dollars. That's when he decided he couldn't be there anymore, always seeing Lucas smile as he glanced at pictures of his family on his desk, always seeing the disappointment in his dad's eyes.

So he'd done something out of character, taking a vacation, catching a commercial flight to San Francisco and heading for wine country where he could clear his mind and then return to New York in better working order. At the airport, he'd rented a modest SUV and hit the road, trying to find a place where no one knew his name, where they couldn't join in his suspicions that he would never change.

Some men didn't turn out to be family guys like Lucas, who'd discovered his inner goodness through someone who loved him.

Worse yet, David had realized on the flight over that something else bothered him. He was no longer the esteemed son of the family, and although his first instinct was to chalk up his resulting unease to simple jealousy of Lucas, it went even deeper than that.

The notion actually pulled at the fabric of his world, tearing it until it didn't hold any longer. After all, who was he now, if not the "successful son"?

Since he'd last talked to his dad face-to-face, there'd been threats from Ford about tracking him down and hauling him back, but Lucas had taken over from there, knowing David wouldn't leave like this unless it was serious.

"I wish you'd tell me what's going on," Lucas had said during their last phone call.

David had assured him that he would check in every day to let them know he was safe—hell, all they had to do was access his careless travel paper trail to know where he was—but he wished they would respect his privacy. He'd said that this was the first vacation he'd ever taken, and Lucas seemed to understand the rest— David was getting his damned head together, and he couldn't do it in New York.

So was his plan for betterment working? And did it include lingering in the market next door to the Suds Club?

Through the window, David saw her walk by. Naomi.

She had a spring to her step as the air blew her curly brown hair and flowered dress. And she was smiling, too, as if thinking bright thoughts to herself.

Somewhere deep in his chest, David's heart curled like a plastic object that been left too long in the sun. Everything seemed to melt ever so slightly, warming him.

He ignored that, telling himself, instead, that he was only reacting to the fact that Naomi was the type of woman Ford Chandler wanted his son to find—a kind woman who came fully loaded with a family.

Lucas, too, had brought home a ready-made brood, and it had led to him winning their dad's heart.

Not that David had intended for that to happen.

Goaded by guilt, David realized that his feet were carrying him away from the apple display and outside. At the Laundromat door, he saw Naomi's dress belling behind her as she entered The Suds Club.

You can have what Lucas has, said the ice man within. *You can be the number one son again by showing Dad you're worthy of someone like her.*

Even if he wasn't.

As David entered the Club, he forced away the unwelcome thoughts. Naomi wasn't a strategy, damn it. She wasn't just another methodical scheme to get what he wanted.

So what the hell was he doing here?

The tang of detergent enveloped him right along with the mumble of pre-soap-opera commercials from the TV. The Club was near-empty today, with only that guy reclining in the same corner with his computer. Naomi was sitting in a little plastic chair in front of the television, clearly waiting for David.

When she spotted him, her face lit up, as if someone had switched on an entire avenue of lights behind her eyes.

He quashed the instinct to look behind him to see if she was acknowledging someone else, then gathered his composure. Just why wasn't it possible for him to deserve that kind of glance from her?

He smiled, and from the way she blushed, he thought that maybe, just maybe, he might have a decent person in him after all if she was responding this way.

"Reporting for duty," he said, sauntering near.

"I knew you would." Naomi gestured to a chair beside her, and he sat. "It's useless to resist the pull of the *Beach.*"

He fought to keep himself from commenting about what had really lured him here. If he couldn't explain it to himself, how could he articulate it to her?

Without preamble, she launched into Soap Opera for Dummies, explaining the basics of the storyline.

But he was barely listening, what with the way her soft mouth formed her words. Her lower lip was fuller than the top one, making him itch to run his thumb over it....

He realized she'd stopped talking, coming to watch him instead, her brows furrowed. But then the show started, and it was a perfect excuse to ignore the awkwardness of being caught. He focused on the TV instead.

What had she seen on his face as he'd fantasized about touching her? What had he just seen on *her* face?

At a commercial break, he stopped her before she could start up with another background exposé of the main characters.

"How long have you been a fan?" he asked, searching for something, anything to say.

"I started tuning in when I was twelve. Every summer after that, I was glued to the TV at noon. My foster mom at the time loved it, too." Naomi's olive eyes lost a bit of their sparkle. "It was one of the only things we ever connected over. A soap opera."

"You were a foster kid?"

"Several times over." She wore a wry grin, but it seemed forced. "Nobody wanted to adopt me because I had a bad attitude."

Once again, something happened to his chest—a twisting sensation that resembled crisped branches getting tangled in a wind.

"You?" he said, motioning toward her light, sprightly

dress and the white Keds shoes she wore. "Surely you're overstating the 'bad attitude.'"

"No, no, not at all. I wore my hair like this." She pushed her wild chin-length curls over her face. "That way no one could look at me. And it drove my parents and teachers crazy. I loved that, because if I could get this kind of reaction out of them, it meant I hadn't totally disappeared."

"Naomi, believe me when I say that you don't escape the eye easily."

His comment had come out effortlessly, without planning or anticipating what a compliment would be worth. It clearly pleased her, as well, because when she slowly brushed her hair back again, her blush had reappeared, pinkening her dusky skin.

One long curl remained over her face, as if it were the lone holdout in protecting Naomi, as if it were the only shield left from years of trying to hide. David stopped himself from reaching out to coax it away from her smooth skin, just so he could see all of her.

"So you were a rebel," he said softly.

"Still am, but in a less obvious way." Her Southern drawl sounded more pronounced, as if this were some kind of shield, too. "I find that subtlety is way more effective than any in-your-face stuff."

"I know what you mean," he said, thinking of how he'd lain low during so many business schemes while, in reality, he'd been pulling all the strings. Subtlety incarnate.

Had his habits become so engrained that they would be impossible for him to change? Was he wasting his time trying?

Maybe if he were serious about changing, he would tell Naomi his true identity right now. He would withstand the inevitable distance that would come between them once she realized that he was one of the richest men in the country. He would sacrifice his anonymity, even though he had never felt so comfortable…or so on his way to finding answers about himself.

Then again, he didn't have any intentions of manipulating her. Not even close. All he wanted was this enlightening, simple interaction before he moved on. If he were planning on staying in Placid Valley, then, yes, revealing everything to her would've been necessary. Yet, he wouldn't be around very long, and he wasn't sure why she needed to know the true identity of this stranger who was merely passing through town.

He wasn't out to hurt her. He would make sure that didn't happen.

The soap opera eased out of its commercials and back into action, but David barely noticed. They kept talking as if the reason for him being here—the excuse of watching *Flamingo Beach*—didn't exist.

"So what brought on the turn from rebel into who you are now?" he asked.

Naomi tilted her head as she considered an answer. "I guess I got sick of myself. Who knows. I turned eighteen and, suddenly, I was on my own, and I realized that the attitude was probably my way of giving my foster parents a reason *not* to adopt me. I'd made sure they were rejecting me because of the attitude I projected and not because of the *real* me. Does that make any sense?"

"Yeah." He was impressed with her self-awareness, at the depth of what she was keeping behind the flowery prints and sunny disposition.

She sighed. "I didn't even *think* about trying to track

down my real parents, either. I don't even have the urge to do it today. I always figured my dad left my mom because he didn't care and my mom dumped me for the same reason. That's their cross to bear, and if they want to look for *me* one day, well best of luck to them."

Her voice had gone thick, and he started to touch her arm. But she straightened just before he moved, and he took that to be a signal that she didn't want sympathy. That she'd lived all her life without it and wasn't about to tolerate any now.

"Hence," she added, "I'm the mixed bag you see before you."

That area around his heart was heating up again. "You're one of a kind, Naomi. Do you know what a commodity that is?"

She looked away, as if the compliments were too tough to take. "I suppose I do."

He wanted to know more. Wanted to know what she liked to do now that she was out of the rebel stage. Wanted to know why she'd left her home and come all the way to California without the father of her child.

But then she suddenly started talking about wineries around the area instead, as if veering away from the subject at hand. Maybe she thought she was boring him with all the personal talk. David wasn't sure.

All he knew was that they talked until the soap opera's end credits started rolling and they found themselves in an utterly empty Laundromat.

"I guess Liam couldn't hear the soap over our voices?" she asked. "I hate to have chased him out."

And David hated to leave just because the program was over.

When she rose from her chair, obviously intending to do just that, he stayed seated out of habit. He knew how to use body language to run a situation, and usually, maintaining his position would persuade the other party to remain at the table.

When he realized what he'd done, he stood, too.

Yet Naomi hadn't taken the bait anyway. She'd been waiting for him to follow, a friendly smile on her face.

"Are you off to your job?" he asked.

"Actually, it's my night off, but it's errand day. A trip to the bank, then to the market to fill the fridge. You know—stuff you don't want to do on vacation. But you? *You've* got some wineries to visit."

"Maybe not today." He didn't want her to leave, not when he was finally getting somewhere in understanding what he needed to do to return to his family with some amount of self-improvement. "I'm thinking of trying out a restaurant that I read about in the paper. Highly recommended. A place over in Novato with family-style New Orleans grub. Would you like to join me?"

Her eyebrows shot up, as if this was the last thing she'd been expecting. And maybe it should've been.

"Don't make me dine alone," he added with a grin that was starting to come so naturally.

When her hand stole over her belly, David guessed what she was thinking. Her baby. Her baby's father.

"Just," he continued, "an extension of coffee. That's all it'd be, Naomi."

And he meant it.

He could tell by her relieved expression that he'd alleviated her concerns. Yet she was still settling into this new town and some companionship wouldn't come amiss.

Yup, if there was one thing David could do, it was read his company.

At the reminder of the David he was trying to leave behind, his grin started to fade. But Naomi brought it back again when she opened her arms, as if surrendering something.

"Sure," she said. "A girl's got to eat dinner, so let's get our grub on."

Even though Naomi had never been to New Orleans, she found that the restaurant, Sullivan's, lived up to all her notions of the city's lively reputation.

It was decorated in gold and maroon, with a staircase leading from the crowded lower floor to a more exclusive loft with intimate tables. Gilded touches, such as the chained light fixtures hanging from the ceiling, made her think of an upscale cathouse where bon vivants came to play. Downstairs, the long tables were piled with dishes such as gumbo, crab cakes, étouffée and jambalaya. However, she was sticking to what would be best for Baby and that meant eating mild, nonseafood items such as Irish stew and a roast beef po-boy that Dave had ordered special from the accommodating kitchen.

Laughter and conversation filled every corner as strangers mingled, bonded by the delicious food.

She and Dave had been seated between a wall and an older couple from Washington, D.C.; the gentleman regaled them with tales of his job as a lobbyist. The discussion almost kept Naomi's mind off her tug-of-warring emotions about having accepted Dave's invitation for dinner in the first place.

Almost.

This is just an extension of "coffee," she kept telling herself. *We're* not *on a date.*

But when the D.C. couple finished up and left, they didn't seem to understand the parameters of Dave and Naomi's relationship.

"You two kids have fun," said the lobbyist, offering a subtle wink as he gave a cheery pinch to his wife's derriere. "Don't do anything I'll be doing tonight."

Um…embarrassing?

As they left, Naomi refrained from gauging Dave's reaction, but she felt his gaze on her all the same.

"Coffee"? Sure, right.

Out of the corner of her eye, Naomi saw Dave lifting his ginger ale to his lips for a drink. He'd ordered the same as her, saying he liked the stuff, even though she suspected he might rather have a beer instead.

A high-end beer, she thought, finally looking up at him and his high-end bearing.

Although he was dressed in a nice khaki shirt and jeans—both from the vintage shop—he still projected an imposing demeanor. It made her wonder again, exactly who he was and what he was about.

"So," he said, setting down his drink as the jitter of silverware and clinking glasses echoed around the room, "our guests didn't let us finish our own conversation from this afternoon."

"The one where I told you about my wild child years? Dave, I was barely interesting enough to all my parents, so why do you want to hear more?"

He leaned forward, resting on his elbows, eyes a

vivid blue that drew her in. "Because, as of right now, you're a mystery, Naomi Shannon."

His use of her last name caused her to realize that she'd never pressed for his. But they wouldn't see each other for much longer, so why did it matter?

Still...

What was he—a detective of some sort? A problem solver in his normal life?

She *did* know that he was a tourist, and this gave her some freedom that she might not have felt with a man who'd be sticking around.

"Okay," she said, leaning forward, elbows on the table, too. "You asked for it."

His grin was barely there, but overwhelming all the same. He was an intent listener, and she wasn't so used to most people actually being intrigued by—and not just *hearing*—what she had to say.

She talked over the noise in the room, picking a piece of lettuce out of her side salad to munch on.

"I'm not such a mystery, really. I just come from a very uptight small town where people were all too willing to believe that I was still a shady person. It's my fault for encouraging them to think that way, but... Well, the last thing I wanted was for my child to grow up being called names and having to deal with preconceived notions. Small town people don't forget the reputations of sweet innocent little babies' mommies, you know. To have my son or daughter suffer the gossip..."

Her throat tightened. She'd been willing to do anything—even risk a new life in a new place—for her child. Kane's Crossing definitely kept their community in check. Her baby deserved a chance to live a gossip-free existence away from the scandal Naomi had created by becoming an unwed mother.

"You're alone in this?" Dave asked, lowering his voice as the room started to clear, diners leaving and laughing while holding their stomachs. "The father...?"

"The father isn't going to be involved in our lives."

Silence sat between them like a last, heavy course that they hadn't ordered.

Maybe he was waiting for her to elaborate, but she couldn't, not even to Dave, who wouldn't be around to judge her.

Finally, he nodded, accepting what she'd given and not asking for more.

Thank goodness, because talking about Bill would only exacerbate the sadness she'd managed to erase earlier when she'd told Dave about her string of foster parents. Like them, Bill ultimately hadn't wanted to take her in, either.

Was she that unlovable?

No, she thought. Naomi's child would adore her because she already loved him or her so much. She wasn't alone at all.

"What you did takes courage," Dave said. "Moving away and coming out here on your own with a child to care for."

"Does it?" Naomi laughed, a brittle sound. "And here I thought it would take more guts to have stuck around Kane's Crossing."

"Why is that?"

This she could tell him, because it was over and done with, a bump in the road behind her. "My wild days brought all kinds of nicknames on me, and you can only guess what it's like being a foster child among more stable kids. They liked to call me 'trash.' Creative, huh?"

"Trash." Dave's gaze took on a thoughtful darkness.

But she knew it wasn't because he was judging her. If that were so, she would start feeling that pit of emptiness inside. She would see the superiority in the lines around his mouth or the narrowing of his eyes.

Actually, it was as if he were angry for her sake.

"You," he said, "are as far away from 'trash' as a person can get. Believe me."

For the first time in her life, she felt removed from that label. Dave made her feel as if she'd always been smiley, positive and determined. "Trash" didn't even seem like a possibility with him looking at her this way.

She put down her fork, realizing that she was still holding it. "I've been on the outside for so long that I'm not sure what it's like to be in."

"I hear you."

She'd spilled a lot of beans, so she was going to make him do the same. "Why do you say that?"

He paused, leaned back, anchoring his hands on his thighs. It was as if he were weighing what he could tell her and what he couldn't.

Ultimately, he shrugged, indicating that what he was about to say didn't matter so much. "You had foster parents, so you felt alienated in a lot of ways. I have a father who's been around the marriage block more than a few times and a mom who divorced him when I was yea-high. They traded me off to each other while I was growing up until I finally decided to stay with my dad. It wasn't so much a personal decision, either, as much as a…well, a more realistic one. I was interested in his business pursuits. I wanted to learn what he did for a living from the ground up, even at a pretty young age, but there were times I felt…"

"Removed?"

"Yeah, removed." He paused. "But I moved on and concentrated on succeeding."

So he was some type of businessman. "How serious of you. Were you the kid who wore suits everywhere, even to school?" she asked jokingly.

"Not everywhere." He grinned, but it didn't seem right. It seemed more like a gesture designed to make her think he didn't mind being a serious-minded child in yet another broken home.

He seemed to catch on to her sympathy, and he continued, as if to swerve around it. "Life's been kind to me, though. My mom and I are still on good terms. I've had a…strong relationship with Dad, too. Nothing to complain about."

Abruptly, he tossed his napkin onto the table, as if to end this discussion. He glanced about the room, and that's when she noticed they were the last customers, and the waitstaff was clearing tables around them.

"We shut the place down," he said, rising and moving around the bench to stand by her. "I hardly noticed."

He held out his hand to aid her in standing. Her first instinct was to avoid his help. Uh-huh, she was that scrappy because she was so used to doing things on her own. Bill had even taken a while to get used to her independent streak. It'd been that way with a lot of her boyfriends, come to think of it.

But, this time, she took a man up on his offering.

She slipped her hand into Dave's, feeling the texture

of rougher skin against the smoothness of hers. After she got to her feet, she allowed her grip to linger in his. Truth to tell, it felt too good to let go.

"Thanks for getting me out of the apartment tonight," she said softly. "With my friend Carissa gone, it gets a little empty in there sometimes."

"Why deal with the emptiness?" he asked, smiling a true smile this time. A whopper that almost knocked her to the ground.

Friends, she reminded herself. *Just friends.*

All too aware of his flesh against hers, she slid her hand out of his, and he got out his wallet to pay the bill. She insisted on contributing her share, but he managed to talk her out of it without her even realizing he'd done so.

Naomi thanked him. He nodded, enclosing his change in the provided leather bill folder. She noticed that the money was crisp, just as *he* had been yesterday when they'd met at the Laundromat, before their visit to the vintage store.

They strolled outside into the parking lot, as if unwilling to call it a night. At least, that's how she felt. The atmosphere was too mild and clear, the stars too bright to waste.

Dave opened his SUV door for her and, somehow, the giddy feeling of being on a real date overcame her.

Maybe it was those stars.

Or maybe it was the look on his face, as if he'd been thinking that tonight had gone beyond "coffee," too.

Chapter Five

He wanted to kiss her.

Throughout dinner, he hadn't been able to take his eyes off Naomi, her soft gaze capturing his, her lips shaped into a smile that dug into him even right now under the moonlight.

As he took her hand to guide her into the passenger seat, a zing of awareness flew up his arm, spreading heat through him with such speed that his mind raced to catch up.

His chest, his stomach, down to his belly and below...

Heartbeat thudding, David just stood there, hardly knowing what was happening. All the college degrees and business deals in the world hadn't prepared him to negotiate this, whatever it was.

He'd never felt so unbalanced in his life.

Naomi was watching him now, lips slightly parted,

the wind toying with her dark curls. She seemed as confused as he was.

But she also appeared more than interested to see what might happen next.

When she swallowed hard, David couldn't stop himself from reaching up, resting his fingertips against her cheek. Her skin seemed as soft as the flowers that graced his office lobby daily—petals that fell to the carpet and were picked up by the staff to preserve appearances. He had never stopped to touch those flowers; it was only now that he realized how good they might have felt if he'd just bothered to notice.

"Dave?" she asked, and he didn't know if she was warning him off or asking him to continue.

Experimentally, he ran his fingers down the slope of her cheekbone. Sensation skated over his flesh, making his breath lodge in his chest.

As his touch drifted down near her mouth, her eyes fluttered closed, her lashes like black fans over her skin. The reaction made her seem so vulnerable, causing a surge of an unidentifiable emotion to well within him.

No, wait. He knew what it was. Protectiveness.

Their dinner conversation had gotten to him, the stories about her being "trash." He wanted to know what the father of her baby had done to disappoint her, wanted to know his name so he could give an identity to the jerk he wanted to knock upside the head.

But even though David didn't know her well, he knew enough to realize that she would probably prefer to wage her own battles.

Her eyes opened and, this time, there was a world of

heartbreaking questions in her gaze, making him wonder if all her apparent chutzpah was just another act, like the rebel she'd been in her youth.

Yet…no. There was a certain strength in the way she looked at him, too.

"What are you doing, Dave?" she whispered, as if challenging him. Or maybe, again, she was gracefully telling him to back off.

Why couldn't he read her *now?* He wasn't used to getting scrambled up like this.

"I have no idea what I'm doing, Naomi. No idea at all."

She hesitated, moonlight playing over her dusky skin.

"The way you're looking at me right now… I'm not so sure anymore if you're the harmless, nice guy I assumed you were. You are a good guy—aren't you?"

Was she actually asking if he was anything like the man she'd left behind in Kane's Crossing? Was she asking if David was just as much of a bastard as the father of her baby?

Maybe David used to be a bastard. But he took no satisfaction in that reputation now.

Could he be a good guy?

Brushing his thumb under her bottom lip, he nodded, hoping she'd still see the type of man he yearned to be. A guy who didn't twist people's lives around to suit his own needs. A guy who could make up for what he'd done to Lucas and Alicia.

A guy who deserved to be a favorite son again once he returned to his family.

And, because he wanted to earn that so much, he lowered his hand, intending to help her into the car and go on his way.

But before he could manage that, she stood on her tiptoes, catching his mouth with hers.

Shocked pleasure roared through him at the unexpected contact, at the pressure of her lips, warm and moist.

Coffee? Friends?

Something like lightning shot through every limb, bolts of a craving that were tearing him apart.

Urged on, he touched her face again, then slid his hand down until his thumb rested at the base of her throat. There, her heartbeat pounded, transferring flickering images to his brain, like a strobe light mangling his sight, decimating all rational thought.

Don't take advantage, he kept trying to tell himself. *Be that good guy.*

But when she pressed her body against his, breasts to his chest, hands buried in his hair, David started to lose it. His groin, now nestled against her belly, surged with the hot blood banging there.

Helpless, he slipped one arm around her, the other hand moving to the back of her head where he twined his fingers in that gorgeous, bohemian hair. He sought more, deepening the kiss as she parted his lips with her tongue.

Her kiss grew demanding, her breath choppy.

When she made a low, needful sound in her throat, David coasted his mouth there, feeling the thud of her pulse in her neck through his lips, nipping at her until she winced.

Good guy...

"Dave," she said, hands tightening until she gripped his hair. "Oh, Dave..."

Hearing the name rattled David. He paused as she

gasped for breath. He also caught the slam of the restaurant door, the surge of voices.

He panted against her skin, her soft skin that smelled of freshness and temptation, and then backed away, holding her hands in his.

"I'm sorry," he said. "I didn't mean to—"

"Sorry?" She cocked her head, gaze unfocused as her chest rose and fell. "Sorry because…?"

She searched for words, and he wanted to help her, he really did, but he didn't know quite what to say, either. He hadn't been out to seduce her at the beginning of the night. All he'd wanted was the promise she held: the glimpse into another life. The goal of being Dave.

But he knew that was wrong. He genuinely wanted her, pure and simple, man to woman. He'd known it from the second he'd first seen her.

David would've taken advantage of the situation, but *Dave* sure as hell wouldn't.

"I'm apologizing," he said, still holding her hands, "because I didn't plan for tonight to go this way. I just wanted to be around you, Naomi. To talk, to laugh. That's all."

"That's a—" She stopped, suddenly seeming amused rather than angry. "Well, it sure looked like you wanted to kiss me. That's what made me lose my head. Just for a second. A tiny little second."

The voices in the background floated off. Car doors slammed.

"I did want to kiss you," he said. "It's all I could think about."

She averted her gaze, and he immediately regretted being so forthcoming. He wasn't used to being direct, at least out of the office. Now he knew why he'd never made a habit of it. Baring his emotions could hurt.

Pushing back her hair, Naomi glanced at the car door, just over his shoulder. She'd become distant these last few moments, now that their kisses had cooled.

"I don't know what I'm doing," she said. "You're in town for vacation, so I guess that made it all right to lay one on you."

"But," he continued for her, "this doesn't mean we need to…"

God, where was the businessman who could present the facts?

"Right," she said, saving him the discomfort of elaborating. "We don't need to pursue it further. We already got the awkwardness of wondering when or if a kiss might happen out of the way, and now we go back to having that coffee."

Knowing that this thing—whatever it was—with Naomi wouldn't go beyond one kiss, he offered his hand again to help her into the SUV.

But, this time, she didn't accept the gesture, choosing instead to climb into the cab all on her own.

"Pop quiz," Naomi said to Mei at The Suds Club the next afternoon, just before the soap started. "What would *you* do about my wandering hormones?"

Her friend leaned against the dryers as someone else's load slapped against the metal. "I don't know. On one hand, I realize you feel strongly about keeping life simple until you've got it under control. I can see why you'd want to stay out of getting involved with a man at this point."

"So I should stay away from Dave. No calling him or bugging him or inventing excuses to see him again."

"Well…" Mei tapped a slender finger against her chin. "You've already told me that he's not a long-term threat to your well-being, either. He's a traveler, so maybe a little fling would please those rampant pregnancy hormones that are skittering through your body."

As Naomi started to argue that, Mei held up her finger.

"Please," she said. "I remember the raging fires that can consume some pregnant woman very, very well. When Travis used to come home at night—during those days when he was more of a husband and less of a man obsessed with saving the world—I was on him like sugar on a cookie. But that, of course, was before everything…"

She let the sentiment drift, leaving Naomi to fill in the blanks. Mei didn't need to explain about her marriage falling apart. How his choices had broken her heart.

Naomi watched Mei to gauge that she was okay, and it seemed her friend was. Only a trace of anger and hurt betrayed her feelings.

Mei seemed to realize that, and she put on a smile, bending down to help Naomi retrieve her clothing from the dryer. "So go on. You were talking about hormones, kisses…?"

Naomi knew the best thing to do was to keep talking, get Mei's mind off her own problems. "Maybe that was the thing," she said. "Out there in the moonlight, after he seemed so interested in everything I had to say, after I'd driven myself bonkers imagining what it might be like to kiss him—"

"He's not bad to look at, all right—"

"I got a little enthusiastic. I saw that kissing expression

on his face, and I don't remember much after that. You know exactly what I mean by the kissing expression."

"Oh, sure. It's that intense moment when you can read it in his eyes. What fond memories I have of it." Mei grew pensive, tucking a strand of long dark hair behind her ear and glancing away.

Naomi rested a comforting hand on her friend's arm. Mei smiled, telling Naomi she was fine. Just fine.

"And then," Mei said, obviously making an effort to get back to the original subject, "what happened after the kiss?"

"Then I guess I gave in to my emotions." Naomi sat down, hesitating in thought. "It's weird, Mei. I haven't felt this way before, not even when I was younger. It's like I can barely control myself around him, and that's not like me."

"Maybe this is saying something, Naomi."

Maybe it was. She felt it in her bones: Dave really was a good man. A gentleman who hadn't wanted to take advantage of her. True, she'd been miffed when he'd cut off their passionate kiss, but that was no doubt because she'd previously been so insistent on keeping things mellow and he was respecting her wishes.

"So what are you recommending then?" Naomi asked.

"Do what you want to do." Mei lifted her hands in a shrug. "Once he's out of town, you'll be in here saying to me, 'Mei, I sure wish I'd done things differently.' He's temporary, Naomi. He's a distraction you can enjoy before going back to real life. A perfect situation for your needs."

As Mei took a seat before the TV, Naomi wondered how much of her friend's take-what-you-can-get attitude had to do with tension in her marriage.

Still, she liked what the other woman had to say. No denying that.

At any rate, as the soap started and she, too, sat down, she began to wonder why it was that leaving Bill hadn't caused this much consternation.

The weekend dragged by on pins and needles for David.

On Saturday, he told himself that he wasn't going to pop up at The Suds Club again to wait around for Naomi to show. So he drove to the Russian River, sampled some wine that tasted like water for all the thought he was putting into appreciating it, then drove back home after a long dinner by himself at a nearby roadside joint—a new, odd experience.

On Sunday, he'd woken up, aimless, wondering what he would do now. So he took out a map, tracing routes with his finger, indecisive. He'd ended up puttering around his new hotel—a more generic place that a guy like Dave would've chosen. He'd gone to the pool, read an action novel that had nothing to do with business, then consulted the map again.

Should he move on from Placid Valley?

Or should he just stay for a while more?

But there was no reason to do that. It pissed him off that he was hoping for a phone call from Naomi. For some kind of word.

The next morning, after another long meal alone at a city restaurant that the concierge had suggested, David finally decided to head out.

And, naturally, that's when Naomi called on the hotel phone.

"Hello?" he answered, pulse awakening. He tried to tamp down his pleasure, his anticipation, but he wasn't so successful.

However, it kind of made him happy, not being afraid to show his excitement at hearing from her.

"Hey, Dave."

She sounded almost shy, and that useless, protective urge consumed him again.

"How was your weekend?" he asked. Small talk. Good stuff.

"Not much happened except for a call from my roomie. She's taking a breather in Rome. What a life, huh? I guess I'm giving her the freedom to goof off because I'm here taking care of her plants and watching her place. *Not* that I'm complaining at all."

"The way you said Rome… It's as if you'd love to visit."

"If only."

He wished he could tell her that he had the means to make that happen. Wished for a lot of things when it came to Naomi.

"Listen," she said, "I'll bet you're wondering why I'm calling."

"It crossed my mind."

"Well, truthfully, I need a favor. You don't have to do it, mind you, but I thought I'd give it a shot."

A favor, huh? "Shoot, then."

She laughed—a fresh, uplifting sound. He pictured her lips again: how they had pressed against his mouth with such feverish need the other night.

He averted the phone and blew out a breath as she continued.

"I'm limited on transportation. Sold my hunk of junk in Kane's Crossing for about a thousand dollars, and Carissa's car is kaput. I've just been walking most places, like the Laundromat."

"How about your job?"

"Within walking distance, too, but I catch a ride home every night from a girl who works at a clothes store next door. Pregnant gals need exercise, and walking's just the thing. I'll take public transportation once my tummy gets bigger, and I could take it now, too, but I don't see a good reason to deny myself a good stroll."

"And where do you want me to drive you?"

Another laugh from Naomi. Another thrust of desire through David's belly.

He calmed himself, knowing that he wouldn't be getting more kisses. But, again, that wasn't the only reason he yearned to be around her. She meant a lot more than the physical.

"I've got an appointment with my new obstetrician this afternoon," she said. "I know it's short notice, but if you had time to take me…"

"When do you want me to pick you up?" Damn him, he was already on his feet, reaching for his wallet on the nightstand.

"Say one o'clock? In front of The Suds Club?"

That's right—she would've arranged an appointment after her soap.

"You can depend on me," he said, meaning it.

Hoping he could live up to the promise.

After they disconnected, he found himself too distracted to do much but go down to the exercise room, work off some pent-up energy, then take another shower.

When he got back to his room, he found that both his dad and Lucas had left voice mails on his cell phone, so he made quick work of returning the messages.

During the call back, only a hint of the old David returned: brusque, all business, refusing to divulge exactly where he was when Ford Chandler threatened to come out after him.

He was making such progress on his own, David thought. Couldn't his dad get that?

Lucas, who was obviously in the same room with their father, calmed Ford, then got on the line to persuade his brother to hurry back.

After saying he would return soon and advising them to stop worrying, David disconnected, thinking of how the tables had turned with his brother.

Not two years ago, in the midst of David's Machiavellian scheme to acquire a key company for The Chandler Corporation, Lucas had been just as addled as David was now. According to plan, Lucas had married good-girl Alicia to attract positive media attention and convince Tadmere and Company to sell. But then Lucas had done the unthinkable, falling in love with the woman who had no idea that she was merely a pawn in their strategies.

David had tried to talk his brother out of falling for her—the marriage was merely business, he kept saying. But Lucas hadn't listened.

Now Lucas was the favored son who was giving orders to David, and *that* was profoundly startling.

Deep down, he bristled, his hunger to become *the* son, *the* success of the family—not the screwup—emerging again.

By the time David pulled up to the curb in front of the Laundromat, Naomi was already waiting, wearing a light, loose skirt and blouse that were perfect for the mildly sunny day. She waved as he stopped the SUV, got out and went around to her side to guide her into the cab.

Then, when they were settled in their seats, she drank a long swig from her water bottle before giving him directions. He merged with the traffic, hands tight on the steering wheel as he fought to forget Lucas and their father.

"I'm so happy you could help me out," she said, turning to face him, the seat belt firmly around her.

Happy. David had significant doubts if he would ever be able to make a woman truly joyful. If he always needed to be the number one prince of the family, how was he ever going to have enough room for devotion to someone else in his life?

Even though he knew he shouldn't, he glanced over at Naomi. God, he hoped he wasn't just using her in his own game of self-improvement.

But when he focused on her, a tiny explosion shattered him.

That kiss. The way his world had rocked when her lips had touched his…

Being with her *had* to mean more.

And that realization scared the life out of him.

He tried to swallow, to coat a throat that had suddenly gone dry, but it was tough. The new-car smell of the rental SUV made the air oppressive, made it almost impossible to get a good breath into his lungs.

She seemed to note his silence, and she turned toward the front instead of facing him. Great—where the hell was *Dave* now?

Naomi took another deep drink of her water. He wondered if he should put on the radio.

Just as he was about to, she spoke.

"I guess I'm pretty nervous about this appointment. I shouldn't be, but there it is."

At the blessed small talk, his grip on the steering wheel loosened ever so slightly. "This can't be your first checkup."

"No, I'm more than a couple months along, so I had my first one in Kane's Crossing. That's when I got the confirmation of the pregnancy. Shortly after that, I left town."

Again, she allowed the rest of her story to dangle.

Instead of continuing, she angled toward him, as if testing to see if his mood had improved. "This is the first time I'm seeing my obstetrician here in Placid Valley, though." She took a piece of paper from her purse, scanned it, then pointed ahead. "You're going to want to take a right at the next stoplight. Primrose Avenue."

"Got it. So at these appointments…" He tried to recall what his sister-in-law had gone through with one-year-old Phoebe. "Are you getting an ultrasound? Or is it too early?"

"Oh, no, it's not too early. I'll be doing my first one today. Dr. Richards wants to verify my due date and get acquainted with me and Baby. There'll be forms for me to fill out once I get there, so I'm not sure how long all this will take…."

"That's okay. I have no appointments myself."

He felt, rather than saw, her smiling at him. With a quick glance, he took in her obvious appreciation of what he was doing for her. Of how he was handling being a friend rather than a candidate for more kissing.

His veins heated with the flow of blood rushing to places he needed to keep mellow. Hell, all he had to do was think about touching her and it was over.

Soon, they were at the medical complex, riding the elevator to the second floor, then taking care of paperwork. All the while, David stood by Naomi as if he were a part of this event.

But he wasn't. More keenly than ever, he realized that there was something going on here that branded him an outsider.

In so many ways.

Then it came time to wait, which was a strange experience for David since his doctor always made one of the wealthiest men in creation a priority.

It was at this point that David noticed something off about Naomi.

"Hey," he said in response to her screwing and unscrewing the water bottle, which she'd refilled a few times since entering the office. "Are you still nervous?"

"Even worse than before." She exhaled. "I think it's just hitting me. Up until now, I didn't fully realize what was really happening."

David shook his head, not understanding.

Naomi turned a frightened glance on him. "I'm in a new place, without family, without the friends I've known since childhood, and it's all because the father didn't want…"

A nurse interrupted by calling Naomi's name.

Naomi blinked, as if realizing she'd said too much, then got out of her chair and disappeared through the door as if she were thankful she'd been stopped from explaining anything more.

Chapter Six

As Naomi lay on the padded examination table, she nervously touched her bared belly, which felt strained by all the water she'd downed for the transabdominal exam.

Dr. Richards had asked her to pull up her blouse and push down the elastic waistband of her skirt, where a blanket covered her below the hips. Next, a gel would be spread over her belly in order to allow the transducer to run over the skin with ease. Then, thanks to the miracle of technology, she would be able to get her first sight of Baby.

Her heart started pattering again. For the first time, fear was in her bloodstream, now that the full reality of her situation was upon her.

She was all alone, expecting to raise this child. Sure, Carissa had promised to take time off from her flights during the delivery and its aftermath, and Naomi also had friends willing to fly out here from Kane's Crossing to help. Even her new pals at The Suds Club had volunteered for Baby Duty, but Naomi chafed at having to depend on them.

Besides, all those options, as wonderful as they sounded, were only temporary.

Should she have stayed put back in the place she used to call home, where her old friends could've been of more help? Had she made the wrong choice in coming out here?

Dr. Richards, with her dark hair fixed into a low ponytail and glasses propped on her head, hovered above the table and smiled at Naomi. She seemed soothing, as if she knew just what her patient needed to see.

And then, with timing that couldn't have been more perfect, a nurse opened the door and ushered Dave into the small, floral-wallpapered examination room.

As the nurse closed the door behind him, Dave glanced at Naomi, clearly wondering why he'd been summoned.

There. Already, she felt better, just having a familiar face around—even if she hadn't known Dave more than a few days. He seemed genuinely interested in her, and he was *here*. While waiting, she had decided that she needed this more than anything right now.

"After we got started, I asked if it was okay to have you in the room," she said to him. "I'm a little…overwhelmed, I think."

He smiled, reaching over to squeeze her hand. The texture of his skin, the size of his encompassing hold, the warmth of him all settled her down.

"It's a big moment," he said. "I'd want to share it, too."

She tightened her grip on him, tacitly thanking him for not pointing out that maybe she wasn't so darned independent after all. That maybe she needed to stop with all her talk of making it on her own and reach out to others.

Heck, the mommy books that she studied during slow times at the Trinkets shop told her that she should be allowing anyone who was willing to baby *her* to do so. She'd been too stubborn to think that she could accept that up until now.

As if sensing her inner struggle, Dave stroked the hair back from her forehead, his touch calming. They smiled at each other and her breathing smoothed out, even as her heart raced at his touch.

"Thank you," she said softly.

Dr. Richards interrupted the connection, jarring Naomi back to the moment.

"Are you ready to see your child?" the obstetrician asked. Since Naomi wasn't positive about the exact day of her last period, the doctor was determined to use ultrasound to date this pregnancy.

Naomi took a deep breath and let it out as Dave took his cue and stepped away from the table. He seemed uncomfortable in here, as if he were apart from it all, or even in the way.

Even so, he lingered within viewing distance of the monitor, and she folded her finger into her palm, her hand tingling, empty, without Dave there to hold it.

"I'm ready as ever," she said more to herself than the doctor.

Dr. Richards winked at her patient as she stepped closer, then spread the gel over Naomi's belly. Naomi shifted slightly, a little uncomfortable because of her full bladder. It was supposed to encourage a clearer picture of what was going on inside with Baby.

The gel was cool, and Naomi again glanced at Dave, who had shoved his hands in his pockets while watching the procedure closely. Having him keep tabs allowed her to relax more than before. She trusted him, and that was surprising, not only because they were still new to each other, but because she didn't trust many people in general. Not after Bill, especially.

Sometimes she thought that she should've waited to be with her ex but, then again, if she'd done that, she wouldn't have Baby.

A child to love unconditionally. A child who would love her right back.

Dr. Richards had already brought out the trandsducer—a white handheld device wired to the main machine. She slid the curved edge over Naomi's slick belly.

"Please hold your breath," she said.

Naomi followed orders, wondering when this would be over so she could relieve her bladder.

Meanwhile Dr. Richards talked. "Not only are we trying to determine a due date, but we're locating the placenta."

Naomi had also read in her books that the doctor would probably also be checking for any birth defects today.

She let out her breath, trying not to be nervous. "I suppose it doesn't help that we don't know my parents' genetic history, them deserting me like they did."

"That's one of the reasons I called for an ultrasound." The doctor smiled at Naomi again, as if she had no reason to worry.

And when Naomi checked Dave, it was as if he were making it a point to second the woman's optimism. Naomi anchored to his steadiness.

Why worry? She hadn't exhibited any of the red-flag signs mentioned in her baby books. The only difficulty so far was some infrequent indigestion. Even if you counted the ever-tightening clothes, too, she still didn't have any complaints.

Dr. Richards continued scanning. "You've tried hard to diet right, exercise and avoid all the things you should be avoiding, right?"

"Right." Even Bill.

"Here we go," the doctor said. "Look at this."

Naomi tore her gaze away from Dave to glance at the monitor, where a dark blob seemed to dominate the picture. She realized it was her womb, surrounded by what resembled static. And inside that womb…

She pressed her lips together, unable to speak because her chest had constricted.

Inside that womb was Baby, with hints of tiny arms and legs and a head.

And a heartbeat.

Naomi's eyes went hot and watery. "Hi, there," she whispered, the words burning her throat.

She realized that Dave had even stepped forward, an expression of utter wonder on his face. He laughed, and it was the happiest, most surprised sound she'd heard from him.

"Boy or a girl?" he asked.

Dr. Richards laughed. "Can't tell yet." She addressed Naomi, since she'd been told that Dave was a friend and not the father. "You indicated that, when the time comes, you didn't want to know the sex in advance."

"Yes, I'd like to wait until the birth."

Dave spoke up. "Why?"

His passionate tone caught Naomi, and she found him with blue gaze blazing, his skin…flushed?

Yes, it was flushed. That got to her for some reason.

"Why?" she answered. "Because I've never been the type to peek at my presents before they're opened."

"All right." He nodded, breaking into another smile as he glanced back at the monitor. It was as if he couldn't keep his eyes off Baby. "But consider this: the day you learn the sex would be another day to celebrate. For one, you've got the day you learned you were pregnant. That's one party. Two, you learn if you'll have a little boy or girl. Another party. And, three, there's the birth itself. See? One more special occasion."

"I'll think about it," Naomi said agreeably. He had a point, but she liked the idea of being surprised in the end anyway.

Dave seemed pleased, and he grinned at the monitor. There, Baby seemed to shift, raising his or her hands, if Naomi's eyes weren't fooling her.

"Did you see that?" Dave asked.

The tears returned to Naomi's eyes. One trickled down her cheek. "I saw it, all right."

"It's like the baby went 'boo' to us."

"Boo," she repeated. "Like the girl in *Monsters, Inc.*" They sold the character trinkets in her store, so she knew them well.

"Yeah," Dave said. "Little Boo."

As another joyful tear fell, Naomi watched her new friend, touched and more curious than ever.

After leaving the exam room so the doctor could conduct more private business with Naomi, David waited in the lobby, a health magazine rolled up, unread, in his hand.

Not that he could concentrate on it. He kept thinking about Naomi, and how being in that room had opened up yet another side of him.

He loved his nephew and niece, but he'd never experienced anything like this with them. A glimpse of a new life forming. A miracle.

That protective vibe he'd started to feel around Naomi had only intensified because, now, he had more or less met Boo, too. Also, for the first time, he'd seen real trepidation from Naomi. Before today, she'd never revealed the wary single mother who wasn't sure she could handle this pregnancy on her own.

The woman who obviously had a real deadbeat ex.

David tapped the magazine on the arm of his chair as a receptionist called for a waiting patient. Around him, things seemed to move in blurred motion, the room quiet with soft elevator music and a lack of conversation.

But his mind was in chaos. He didn't like that Naomi was in over her head and didn't have a significant other around. Plus, the fact that David had more than enough money to help out bothered him. Should he offer financial aid and ride off into the sunset, back to New York, feeling like a better man?

That didn't sit right, either. He, of all people, had come to learn that riches didn't solve anything. Naomi and her child needed...

What? What could he give her that she would accept?

He tossed the magazine onto a table. Ridiculous, this train of thought. He barely knew Naomi, yet here he was, becoming way too involved.

When she finally emerged out of the examination area, she perked up when she saw him, just as she had in the Laundromat the other day. Something fisted in his belly as he got to his feet.

"I'm all settled," she said, tugging on the hem of her blouse. "We're off and running."

He started walking her out. "So how did it all go?"

They reached the outer lobby, and Naomi headed for the stairs. He almost suggested the elevator—what if she overextended herself?—but he had no business doing that.

Before they descended, she reached into her huge purse, then took out a picture. She smiled from ear to ear while she handed it over.

"After Dr. Richards had you leave, she gave me this. A printout from the ultrasound."

Dave absorbed the sight of Boo, who still had his or her hands raised. Something tight banded in his chest, and it wasn't like the pressure he usually felt weighing down on him, either. No, the sensation actually pulled him together instead of crushing him.

In his mind's eye, he could see a different image: his dad, holding a grandchild David had given him in his frail arms. Ford Chandler would beam a proud look at his youngest son, then say, "This is all I wanted for you, too. A good woman, a family. Just like your brother..."

Naomi continued, her voice quavering slightly. "My due date is April 9—a spring baby. And," she said on a note of apparent relief, "they said everything looks fine."

He could tell that she was worried about anything they might find wrong with her child in the future. Wouldn't stressing about it be bad for both Naomi and Boo?

"Don't concern yourself with what *might* happen,

Naomi. That's out of your control. All you can do now is what you've *been* doing."

When he finally glanced away from the picture, he caught her midyawn.

She waved his narrowed gaze off. "I guess fatigue is beginning to set in. The books all warn about that."

"You have to work tonight?"

"I do the closing shift. No biggie. I'm allowed to sit behind that cash register when I need to, and it's a slow time on a school night."

"And what are you going to do when you get closer to your due date?"

She shut down, as if he'd crossed a line and gotten too involved for someone who was just passing through town.

And she was right.

Descending the stairs, she said, "For a man who seemed likely to crack like an iceberg the first day I met him, you're sure melting right now."

He stayed put. "What do you mean by that?"

"I mean that I know nothing about you, Dave, but there you were, in my exam room, and it seemed right. It was the last thing I would've predicted at first. You didn't seem likely to play the concerned party." She shook her head. "I have no idea what to make of you."

Neither did he. But she'd called out the ice man. Little did she know that he wasn't sure this "melt" would last, if he was capable of permanently warming up.

"Naomi," he said, stopping her progress down the stairway.

She stared back up at him, waiting for him to explain the unexplainable. He tried, though he wasn't about to tell her all the painful details. With her, David didn't exist. Only Dave, and he meant to keep it that way.

"I haven't ever been what you'd call an emotionally accessible man," he said. "I saw my parents fall out of love, and that taught me to be on guard. I saw my mom schedule her life around the affairs she was having, and that taught me to block out the pain. And when my parents divorced, I learned that there's nothing you can't fix by detaching."

Naomi's gaze filled with sorrow, but he put up a hand, unwilling to accept that, even though he knew he needed to learn to deal with feelings most of all.

"Through the years, I could tell how sad my mom was at seeing what her son had turned into. But it didn't matter to me, because I had business to keep me content. I closed deals and secured new acquisitions, and this fulfilled me. It always has, Naomi. Yet…there's got to be more. And I'm trying to find that 'more' right now, on this trip of mine. I'm trying very hard."

She planted her foot on a higher step, but didn't approach him. "Dave, I didn't see any ice in that exam room today. I saw…I don't even know what I saw in there, but it wasn't the man you just described."

"No." He laughed shortly. "If you think you witnessed some kind of family guy emerging, you're wrong. My history doesn't support that illusion."

She obviously didn't understand. No use attempting to persuade her that he might not have it in him to reproduce what he'd felt while seeing her child on that monitor for the first time.

As if to reassure himself, he glanced at the ultrasound image in his hand, and…

The area around his heart seemed to liquefy.

It wouldn't last, right?

He walked down the stairs, offering the picture to her. "How about we go to a store and stock up on anything you'll be needing in the future?"

It was the least he could do before he left. But it did trouble him that he was going back to a David habit: expressing affection through money. He didn't know any other way.

"Thanks, but I can't accept gifts from you." She took the photo and concentrated on tucking it into her purse.

"Naomi." Now his frustration with himself was coming out in rising irritation with her. "Just accept the offer, would you?"

"Why?" Her cheeks were pinkening, her Southern accent thickening. "Because I'm a poor girl trying to make it on my own? Okay, so I had a moment of uncertainty today, but it's gone now. I'm fine. Really."

"For Pete's... Would you just admit that you're going to need help?"

She crossed her arms over her chest, eyes turning a dark, murky shade. "I can do this without a...sugar daddy or—"

"Sugar daddy?" She couldn't have said it with more cutting precision, because that's what he felt like—a rich benefactor who kept his distance but would leave her in the end.

"If you recall," she added, leaning toward him to make her point, "there was sure some sugar the other night."

Oh, he remembered, all right. And it didn't help that she was so close to him now, smelling of that spearmint shampoo or lotion she must've used.

Getting a hold of himself, he circled her, descending the couple of steps it took to bring them face-to-face. A pulse beat in her neck, keeping time to the cadence of his temper…or maybe it was more than that.

Yes, it was desire for her. A longing to feel her skin again, a yearning to taste her. Obviously, an addiction had formed the other night, and one kiss hadn't been nearly enough.

His lips tingled as he lowered his gaze to her mouth. Friends?

Hell, no. They'd become much more than that, connected by a kiss and, now, by what had transpired in that exam room.

But when she hitched in a breath—as if coming to her senses—then brushed past him on her way down the stairs, David wondered if he'd merely been projecting his need for family acceptance onto her.

As she left, a thick coat of ice returned to its place around his heart, canceling out the brightness of what the day had held.

After a silent car ride home, Dave had dropped Naomi off, insisting on seeing her to the apartment door.

She hadn't invited him in. No way, because that might've given her a reason to ask him to stay.

To ask him for more than another kiss.

She'd wanted it so badly on the stairway, and she'd almost leaned over that one, scant, impossible inch to get it, too.

Then her common sense had kicked in. It'd been an emotional day and another kiss would've led to more, and more…until it would be too hard to let go.

And she would *have* to let go when he traveled onward.

But wasn't that the beauty of the situation? That he would eventually leave her without a fuss?

So why not just seize the moment?

She tried to stop torturing herself as she extracted her ultrasound snapshot from her purse. She posted it on the refrigerator with a dolphin magnet her roommate had got from Florida's Sea World, her fingers lingering on the photo.

Her baby's picture—"Boo," Dave had called him or her—rested among all the other magnets from Carissa's trips around the world. Naomi couldn't stop looking at it, hopeful, fearful and joyful all at the same time.

Farther down the fridge, a two-year calendar lay open to September's activities. Naomi forced herself away from the picture to flip the pages to next April, where she wrote down her due date.

Then, yawning, she wondered if she could catch a nap before going into work. As a nice change, she only had a part-time shift tonight, but it didn't seem short enough.

The phone rang, showing a Kentucky friend's number on caller ID, so she answered, putting on the speaker-phone as she decided to just get ready for her shift.

But by the time the call ended, Naomi was sitting on the floor, stunned.

"Bill's back in town from his business trip," her friend had said, "and he's real surprised you left, especially without forwarding information."

So he *had* believed that Naomi would wait for him to get back in town so they could discuss the abortion. Figured.

When they'd first started dating, he'd told her that

he didn't want children, and they thought any birth control issues would be covered by a condom. But, obviously, condoms broke—it wasn't an urban legend. And when she'd found out about the pregnancy, she'd somehow thought that his daddy-urges would kick in at her news, but...no.

What an idiot she'd been.

Her friend had gone on to inform Naomi that Bill urgently wanted to get in contact with her, that they needed to have a heart-to-heart conversation.

Well, Bill would have to keep wanting. Before he'd left on his business trip, Naomi had told him that, if he didn't stay and listen to her, she wouldn't be around when he came back. It angered her that he'd assumed she would hang around for a man who didn't want a child with her.

Luckily, she was one of the few people on earth who didn't have a cell phone, so she wouldn't expect any calls on that end. But it would just be a matter of time before Bill found out she was staying with Carissa and got ahold of her that way.

Boy, she wished she had enough money to get her own place, to refrain from putting Carissa in the middle of this.

Slowly, she got to her feet, walking through the lonely apartment where almost everything belonged to her roommate—except for one item. A vase she'd purchased from Trinkets when she'd first gotten the job. Cheap but cute, it had storks flying around on it, plus a fake daisy that came attached so it could never be lost.

Yours and mine, Naomi thought to Boo. *We don't need all that much, do we?*

She recalled how Dave wanted to go shopping for Boo, how he'd offered to provide much more than Bill ever had.

Then, hardly even thinking of what she was doing, she dialed the phone number for Dave's hotel.

All she wanted was to hear that someone was around, that she wasn't utterly isolated, and reaching out to the man who'd been there for such an emotional moment today seemed like the right choice among so many other wrong ones.

He answered the phone and, though she knew he couldn't have been expecting her, she imagined it was true all the same.

"I'm sorry," she said in greeting.

He seemed taken aback by that. "Me, too, Naomi. I didn't want this to be the way we said goodbye to each other."

Wandering near the fridge, she toyed with the edges of the calendar, focusing on one particular date in September, two days from now.

An excuse to see him again.

As if she needed one anymore.

Chapter Seven

David had been surprised when Naomi invited him to
a post-soap-opera birthday party that was being held for
the daughter of a Suds Club friend.

But he'd said yes without hesitation anyway.

Now, here in this pizza parlor kiddieland, he wondered why he'd been so quick to attend. A separate
group of unknown boys decked in Power Rangers gear
was yelling and throwing foam balls at each other. A
nearby amusement area blasted bells and music. And,
worst of all, he didn't know what to do with himself
around Naomi after their recent disagreement.

What was he to her now? He had no clue, and he
wasn't even sure it was wise of him to be standing here
trying to figure it out while the road ahead of him lay
so open and relatively safe.

Reminded of Naomi, he shivered, his skin coming

alive. She was seated next to him at a table littered with presents, balloons and chunks of half-eaten cake on plates. Children and parents alike urged on the seven-year-old birthday girl to open her next gift, and the pig-tailed sweetheart did just that with enthusiasm.

With the cacophony of ripping paper and video games as accompaniment, Naomi glanced up at David, as if to check on him.

He grinned at her. In spite of his puzzlement regarding just what the hell he was still doing in Placid Valley, he was glad that she'd reached out to invite him here after their disagreement at the doctor's office. It was moments like these when everything seemed clearer: this was a *Roman Holiday* for him, and it didn't matter where he was so much as who he was with.

Thing was, in his version of the Holiday, he would end up a different person, not the same one at all.

Farther down the table, the birthday girl adjusted her plastic crown as she came to the last of her presents. She was the daughter of a woman named Vivian, who turned to Naomi as her child tore into the relatively bulky gift David had secured. He had promised Naomi that he would take care of buying it in his ample time, "splitting" the cost since he was a guest at the party, too.

He just wouldn't tell her that he'd paid for most of it.

Although she had told him exactly what to buy, he had taken liberties, covering the cost beyond what Naomi had given him to spend and hoping she would be pleased by what he had purchased.

Not that he had gone overboard. He had stuck to something the much more modest Dave would've bought: a thoughtful, quality gift. Money hadn't been a factor at all.

"What did Naomi get us?" Vivian said, joking around by rubbing her hands together and grinning maniacally.

Naomi spoke over the noise. "The present is from Dave, too."

Every adult at the table seemed to take great interest in that. David noticed Mei, who was with her young daughter Isabel, exchange a smile with the Hitchcock blonde, Jenny Hunter.

Had Naomi talked about Dave to her friends? A rush of satisfaction zapped through him—temporary yet electrifying.

When the birthday girl tore away the wrapping bit by bit to reveal a small, handcrafted dollhouse, the table went silent.

Naomi trained widened eyes on him, but his gaze rested on the toy, a replica of a Cape Cod cottage. He'd seen it in a window of a boutique in town and, compared to the other houses in the shop, it hadn't been too big or ostentatious. It was even a humble creation by the shopkeeper's standards.

"Thank you!" the birthday girl squealed, immediately exploring the little rooms as the other children gathered round, their mouths shaped into Os.

When the adults came to stare at David again—Naomi first among them—he shrugged.

"I found a great bargain," he said.

Mei laughed, watching her daughter zoom over to the toy to "ooh" and "aah," as well. "You're a better shopper than I'll ever be. Oh, just look at Isabel. She's going to be on me for one of those now, too."

Naomi's saucer-eyed silence ate at him. Was she taken aback because he hadn't gone to the local superstore to get the small, plastic dollhouse she had planned for?

Great, he'd probably wounded her pride because she wouldn't have been able to purchase this type of gift on her own.

Then he saw something even more disturbing in her gaze. Questions that he didn't want to answer.

Who are you, and why do you have so much disposable income?

All he'd been doing was trying to find a high-caliber gift that wouldn't be vainglorious in the least. And he hadn't even been able to manage that small task.

"I never made it to the superstores," he said.

Naomi seemed to catch on to his self-derision, and she smiled. Still, he could see the questions remaining.

"I'm just…surprised that you could find something so lovely for the price," she said. "You did good, Dave. Vivian might even steal that gift from her daughter."

David glanced over to find the mother reverently exploring the tiny house, and he smiled. Thank God. It was good to see the gift bringing out happiness in people.

But then the ice man within interrupted.

You managed to impress them, didn't you? Nice work.

Discomfort took over David. He hadn't been thinking of himself at all when he'd purchased that dollhouse. Yet every person at this party was mulling over how much the toy had cost, weren't they?

Once again, he'd ended up using money to gain self-esteem.

Damn it, did he really have to put this much effort into being Dave?

Naomi stood, resting her hand on his arm, as if reading his disquietude.

"You've got great taste," she said. "I said to buy a dollhouse and you sure did."

He leaned over to her, keeping their conversation private as he spoke into her ear. Curls tickled his mouth.

"It really didn't cost much, Naomi. Believe me."

Not relatively anyway.

Patting his arm, she extricated herself from the constraints of the bench. "Just tell me how much I owe you, okay?"

"Not a penny."

God, this had turned into such a big deal.

Still, as he heard the children—and some of the mothers—cooing over the tiny house furniture, he couldn't help feeling as if he'd done a decent thing. He would learn how to act as if money didn't grow on trees. It might take more time, but he would do it.

Jenny Hunter got out of her seat, too, stretching. "Sharing a birthday gift, huh?"

Naomi gave her a please-don't-talk-anymore glare, and David got the hint. Hell, he wasn't a complete moron. He'd read all the glances in the room that told him everyone was aware there was something more going on between him and Naomi than "just friends."

They probably even understood it more than *he* did.

As Jenny bid everyone goodbye because her lunch hour had gone overtime, David kept his mouth shut. Naomi was awfully quiet, as well. Was she thinking what he was thinking?

That they did seem an awful lot like a couple lately? Ever since he'd shared the ultrasound appointment

CRYSTAL GREEN   103

with Naomi, there'd been a snap of new awareness
between them. Yesterday, when they had met for a late
lunch before she'd gone into work, he had noticed it.
Today, the connection seemed even stronger.

She had to know it, too. Problem was, what did it all
mean?

And how far could it possibly go between them as
long as he lied about his identity?

As the gift-opening session faded to a close, with the
birthday girl exclaiming over every single present now,
Naomi yawned and strolled away from the table, toward
the hyperactive amusement area.

"Time for a break," she said.

"Good idea."

David followed her past all the games and the
children darting from one diminutive ride to the other.
It didn't take long to realize that she was heading toward
an empty back room which was obviously reserved for
a massive party later in the day.

He touched her arm, and she angled against his side,
as if taking some of the burden off her feet. The pressure
of her body against his felt welcome and, as they crossed
the threshold into the private area, he could imagine
entering another room across the country, where his
dad would be sitting and smiling at the sight of David,
so content with Naomi leaning in to him.

Lucas would be happy for his brother, too. His kids
would run across the room, excited to meet Naomi.
David's little niece, Phoebe, would probably point to
Naomi's stomach and repeat one of the only words she
knew over and over.

"Baby? Baby?"

After sitting down, with Phoebe and his nephew Gabriel cuddled near, David would place a palm over the emerging curve of Naomi's belly, just because it felt right. He would want Boo near him, too….

In the midst of the fantasy, a realization shook David.

What about being the number one son? Why wasn't he focusing on *that* anymore?

In present time, Naomi pulled him to a stop in the private room and, gradually, the melody from a mini carousel in the amusement area got louder, more immediate.

When she blew out an exhausted breath, David came to full attention.

"You're really tired," he said.

"Just a little. I didn't sleep so well last night. It's like I have to get up every hour to—" She blushed, as if she'd offered too much information.

He took a wild guess that she was talking about a pregnant woman's tendency to go to the restroom frequently. He'd gotten his own book about babies on yesterday's shopping trip, and he had stayed up last night scanning it.

Vacation reading. That's what he kept telling himself.

Before he knew it, Naomi had teasingly rested her head on his chest near his shoulder. "You're a good pillow, you know that, Dave? Can I rest on you for a minute? All I came back here for was a breath of peace and quiet."

And maybe something more? She seemed to want… What? Comfort?

Affection?

His heart banged, and he wondered if she could hear

it with her ear to his chest the way it was. Her hair brushed his chin, and he was overwhelmed with her scent.

Closing his eyes, he tentatively rested a hand on the small of her back. He felt as if he'd come to a landmark.

He was truly Dave at this moment.

In the background, the small merry-go-round began to play the "Carousel Waltz"—sweet, with an undertow of sad, haunting chords.

When he opened his eyes, he found that he and Naomi were swaying slightly, in a motion that hadn't quite committed to being a full-fledged dance yet.

He put his other hand on her back, and she sighed, doing the same, wrapping her arms around him.

"I wish everything were this easy," she said.

A note of sorrow in her voice kept time with the darker flow of the waltz. He'd noticed this same sadness in her eyes the past couple of days, but she hadn't volunteered what it was about. He kept wondering if he should be asking, if he had any right to.

Before he could risk an inquiry—because that would take things a step further than he should be going—she spoke.

"I got this phone call the other day."

He didn't like how this was starting. "Is that what's been bothering you?"

"Yeah." She held to him a little tighter. "It was a friend from Kentucky telling me that…" She hesitated, then stopped swaying with him. "The father is back."

Since she'd never told David details, he wasn't sure how to respond. "Back from where, exactly?"

She adjusted her position against him, propping her cheek against his arm and averting her face entirely.

"He's back from an extended business trip. I didn't wait for him to return to town because I already knew our relationship was over when he left."

"Wait. You broke up with him while he was on the road?"

"Not really. I did it while he was running out the door because his job was more important than talking about our future. I made it clear we were done, but he just didn't accept that."

David's stomach wrenched. *You're too involved. Leave now before you get in any deeper with her.*

But maybe she was telling him this because she needed some help. Good God, for a woman like Naomi, it was a big step. How could he deny her?

Uneasy, he felt like one of those nameless, fictional gunslingers who came into town, solved a problem, then drifted off with his identity still a mystery.

"Bill's going to try to get ahold of me," Naomi continued. "I just know it."

"How do you want to handle that?" There. It was an invitation, the right thing to do, but David had worded it in such a way that she could turn it down without making a big deal of it.

She shook her head, her face pressing into his arm. He held her closer, protectiveness rising.

"I'm not sure what to do, Dave," she said. "I don't even know why he would care enough to track me down when—" She cut herself off. "It's a long story."

"We've got time."

With every sway of their subtle dance, he was getting in deeper.

But he couldn't help himself.

Naomi waited an instant, as if considering what to say. Then she seemed to give in.

"Bill was a new guy in town," she said, voice low and level. "A very successful sales rep. He traveled a lot and bought a nice house in a new development by the high school. Maybe I thought he would erase that 'trash' label I'd lived with, and that was the attraction. I'm not sure but, for a while, I felt like a different girl. He made me see myself in a better way and didn't seem to care what he heard around town about me. He treated me well, but I knew he wasn't interested in settling down any time soon. I even knew that he wasn't into having children, but I thought I could change his mind about that." She chuffed. "Don't we all think it?"

"So did he end up changing his mind when you told him about the baby?"

"Not even close."

David placed a hand at the back of her head, an instinctive reaction. If this Bill didn't want children, had he asked her to get an abortion or put the child up for adoption? Is that what had driven Naomi away?

Maybe she was too embarrassed to tell him, and he sure wasn't going to wheedle her into doing it. She would relay what she wanted to, and they could go from there.

"I'm so angry at myself for thinking he'd suddenly want to be a dad," she added. "We were careful, too. At least, I thought so. But you know what? I got Boo out of the experience, so why regret it?"

"Exactly." A question had crept up on him. "Do you…think you're angry because you still love the father?"

"Love Bill?" Naomi's laugh was soft, cutting. "Being

away from him now, I'm starting to wonder if I ever did love him like I should've. He's got a silver tongue, that one, and he could charm anyone within range. Including me. I think I *wanted* to be in love. What I mean is, I've spent my life wishing the emotion would somehow find me in one form or another."

Her voice had broken on the last word. Naomi, an abandoned daughter, a constant foster child who'd gone from home to home. Of course she would feel that way.

"Thing of it is," she said, "I've been with two men my whole life—the other one was during high school. After that particular encounter, I realized full and well that rushing into sex was never a good idea, no matter how much I needed to feel close to someone. I told myself not to be needy, not to get myself into trouble because I was dependent on others for emotional feedback. But look how it turned out."

"It turned out that you have a child you're going to adore for the rest of your life. Pretty good deal, I'd say."

Her seemingly relieved sigh warmed his shirt. Warmed his heart, too.

"I did come out the winner, didn't I?" she said. "I just want to make sure that Bill isn't a part of the baby's life because who needs a reluctant daddy to give my child hang-ups?"

"You're right."

As if bolstered, she backed away, still keeping her arms around him while meeting his gaze. "Things will turn out for the best, even if I have to work my tail off to see that through."

Brave words and, once again, David wished he could do more than merely listen to her vent. Strong

Naomi didn't expect any man to take up where this Bill had left off.

Not even him.

But his body was telling him differently. He desired to take the place of a boyfriend in the most intimate sense. The clenching of his gut testified to that. So did his thundering blood, screaming to a groin that was tightening by the second because of her proximity.

Just the smell of her—a primal stoking of his senses—was enough to get him going. With her curves rounding into his, with her skin giving off such heat, he couldn't help his body's reaction.

He wanted to lean over, just a whisper, and kiss her. Comfort her. He'd been aching for it during a string of nights now, and he was about to give in.

For a sizzling second, the air seemed to fry.

Electric, hot, hungry…

Take what you want, said his ice man. *What's stopping you?*

The sound of the persona he was trying to leave behind jarred David.

He cooled off by doing the oddest thing possible—stepping back and squeezing her shoulder, neutralizing the moment.

God, he wanted to kick himself.

Confusion took over her expression. She clearly hadn't expected this reaction from him after the look he'd just laid on her. And when her eyes filled with something close to anguish, he wished he could punish himself for bringing that on her.

A rejection, he thought. She believed he was rejecting her, just as her parents and Bill and everyone else had done.

But David would make it up to her, no matter what he needed to do in the little time he would still be in town.

Atonement was necessary.

It was everything.

That night, Naomi sat behind the register at Trinkets pricing a new shipment of fairy figurines that had arrived a few hours ago. She was on the closing shift alone, and business was dead, leaving her with only the Celtic harp soundtrack as company.

She yawned, smoothing a sticker on the figurine's base. This afternoon had tapped her out. First, the party, where Dave had surprised everyone with that dollhouse. Though it wasn't huge in size, it was obviously hand-made and therefore expensive. He said he'd got a real deal, but…still. She had wondered just how well-off he really was to have been able to afford such a gift for a stranger's daughter.

A terrible thought caught up with her: was he deliberately being cagey about his true identity? Was he an affluent married businessman on some kind of fun jaunt away from responsibility?

No, that didn't sound like Dave. Even so, she had to wonder. If it did turn out that he was pulling the wool over her eyes in some way, she would never forgive him.

And there was something else bothering her, too. If he was wealthy in real life, what must he think about her "trash" stories? Was he just being too polite with her to act as if he noticed that she was inferior?

Why would he even want to be around her?

Jeez, his dollhouse had even served as a hit to her pride. She had asked him to buy a cheap toy because she couldn't afford more and, when he'd shown up with the Cape Cod cottage, the gorgeous object had reminded her about her financial status.

She really didn't have enough for Boo, much less another child who was having a birthday.

As she continued pricing the knickknacks, an hour seemed to fly by with no customers to interrupt her work. She had a lot of time to think about so much more, too, including spilling her guts about Bill to Dave. She'd been too ashamed to tell him about Bill's request for an abortion. It'd seemed too personal, too much as if Bill had asked her to remove something she already loved about herself.

She was just about to set the figurines out for display when the man she couldn't stop thinking about walked through the store's entrance.

At the sight of him, dark blond hair so neatly clipped, blue eyes shining, smile emerging, she almost dropped a dancing fairy.

She clutched at it, trying to forget how he had so obviously wanted to kiss her again earlier. How she'd wished for it heart and soul until he'd backed off. His reaction had made her feel like an abandoned girl, although she couldn't blame him for keeping his distance when she couldn't decide, herself, what to do with him.

"Were you bored enough to explore the mall tonight?" she asked, lungs squeezing together so she couldn't talk quite right.

"I thought I'd just come here to see what all the fuss was about."

He glanced around at the shelves and shelves of figurines, including Precious Moments and Harmony Kingdom. Collector dolls lined the walls and crystal sun-catchers reflected the light. Scented candles lent an olfactory rainbow to the surroundings, too.

Raising a brow, he said, "So this is Trinkets."

His tone sounded odd, as if there were more to the comment than she would ever know.

"You have a few in New York," she said. "They do really well there with tourists and, of course, collectors."

It seemed as if this were the last thing he wanted to talk about. Thus, all man-of-action-like, he walked over and took the figurines from her grasp.

"Where do these go?" he asked.

The only thing she could think to do was answer. "Um, there?"

After spotting the near-empty glass shelves where she was pointing, he headed over to deposit the fairies, stocking the old ones toward the front and the new ones behind in proper order.

"Why don't you sit down and direct me," he said, going to the counter and grabbing more figurines. "I'm here to work, so put me to good use."

She merely blinked at him. "What?"

"I hear labor is good for the soul." With a low laugh, he stocked some more. "Actually, I got restless in that hotel room, so I figured expending some energy here would benefit us both."

She didn't feel right, just standing there doing nothing for her salary, so she went behind the counter, got out a box of tangled sun catchers, then sat down and proceeded to unknot their strings.

The Celtic harp plucked at her nerves as he continued his strange task. How many people had ever shown up out of the blue to help her like this?

Who was this guy?

"Dave?" she asked.

While adjusting a line of cartwheeling fairies, he glanced at her in inquiry.

"I'm wondering…" First questions first. "How long are you planning to be in Placid Valley?"

He paused long enough for her to see his Adam's apple working with a swallow. Then he turned to resume stocking. "I haven't decided. My plans are open-ended."

"How open-ended? What I mean is, don't you have to get back to your job? Or…anything else?"

Yeesh, could she be any more obvious while asking about a girlfriend or—God help her—anyone even more important?

He caught on, of course. "I'm as single as they come, Naomi, so I'm not gallivanting around on a wife or a significant other. My job, on the other hand? That's definitely waiting for me. And so are my father and brother, who work with me."

Phew—a solid answer. But it didn't explain why he kept himself at a distance most times, even though she supposed it had to do with that "icy" nature he'd talked about before.

But she wasn't satisfied yet.

"What do you do for a living?" she asked.

"I told you." He stood back, admiring his labors, hands on hips. "Business."

"There're all kinds of businesses." Bill had been in "business," too, and she wondered if all of his type were such workaholics.

"Okay, then," he said. "Acquisitions. Mergers. That sort of thing."

"You don't sound so enthused about this."

His gaze drifted to the floor, where he stared at the carpet for a moment. "I suppose I'm not." Then he made a "who knew?" face and came back to the counter for more figurines.

Encouraged by the flow of information, she got ready to ask every question she'd been storing up. She wasn't sure just how much she should expect, even though their relationship had been getting stronger day by day.

"And your brother?" She picked at a particularly stubborn knot in a sun-catcher string. "Is he mergers or acquisitions?"

"He's the boss right now. He's everything."

Dave got a look on his face as if he missed his brother terribly.

"Are you close?" she asked. "You and your brother?"

"Close?" Dave seemed to measure the word. "*Close* is a very subjective way to put it."

"Don't waltz around the issue, please."

He apparently appreciated her spunk. "Lucas and I always got along well while growing up. He's actually my half brother, older, from a different mom. But both of us lived with Dad, and there was that competitive thing most brothers have. I was the brains and he was the face in every situation, even when we grew up and I worked full-time for my father. Lucas, though..." Dave shook his head. "He wasn't so concerned with work until recently, when he asserted himself and became rather good at it."

"So are you close?"

Dave rubbed at his chin, a strained smile threatening his mouth. "I guess you could say we are. He got married, and the dynamics between us changed. I like being around his kids, his family. They lend a lot of…perspective."

"And is that why you went on an aimless vacation by yourself. For some perspective?"

Dave only offered a cryptic raise of the eyebrows, and she accepted it. She'd dug pretty far tonight and had gotten some good stuff. Besides, this was supposed to merely be a fling, not a commitment.

If she could actually *get* Dave to fling with her.

As he finished stocking the shelves, she allowed herself to take him in: his wide shoulders, the muscles in his arms, the fantasy of feeling his length against hers. Heat rose to her skin like flame tickling the surface, then licking downward.

Touching her, priming her.

Making her want him more than ever.

Chapter Eight

The next day, bright and early, David rode the elevator to Naomi's third-story apartment, hefting one of two boxes that contained a "light assembly required" cradle under his arm.

He propped that next to her door, then went back down to his car to fetch the other box, then a tool kit he'd picked up at a nearby hardware store as well as muffins from the bakery down the street.

There was a certain easiness to his steps, but maybe being useful did this to a man.

Not that he hadn't been important in his own way back in New York. But, here, he wasn't affecting numbers in a report. With Naomi, there were profits of a different sort.

He mattered on a personal level now.

To someone he'd come to really care about.

Knocking at her door, he knew she would be expecting him to merely bring over breakfast—nothing more—since he'd called ahead of time. Yet, when she answered, he realized that he hadn't really been prepared, himself, to encounter her again.

Seeing her standing there, dressed in a T-shirt, white capri pants and fuzzy pink slippers, it felt as if he were caving in, like a building imploding to make way for a new, improved structure.

As always her eyes were bright while she greeted him. "Muffins from the neighborhood bakery. As I said before, you've got the best taste."

He still hadn't caught his breath enough to say much, so he only nodded. Her hair was wet, obviously from a shower. Even from across the threshold, he could smell her scent, her skin.

She invited him in, relieving him of the muffins. As she spotted the tool case, she quirked a brow.

"Before I stopped at your store last night," he said, "I wandered around that mall and came across a baby shop. I got curious about what was inside and found something Boo might really like."

What he didn't add was that he'd unfortunately found himself acting like his old persona, as well, checking out the mall's slow traffic and determining whether or not Trinkets would fare better in a strip mall rather than an enclosed one. Coming upon the baby store had been a welcome relief, reminding David of his new priorities. Shopping for Naomi had even been a little fun.

As she kept watching him, clearly curious, he set the tools on the floor and went back outside to grab both boxes for the cradle, then nudged the door shut behind him.

"Dave," she said, gently chiding him. "What did you buy?"

"The saleslady said it's a 'white scalloped cradle.' Handcrafted. Iron, with decorative castings. I couldn't resist."

"I appreciate it, but…" She didn't seem totally convinced, and he found her gaze straying to the picture of the cradle on one bulky box.

He smiled and tilted the image toward her for a better look. "I've still got the bedding in the SUV, but I'll deal with that later. In the meantime, how about breakfast?"

With one last okay-you-won-*this*-time look at him, Naomi went about setting out the muffins and pouring orange juice.

Directing him to the bedroom she was using, she tore into a carrot bran muffin as he transferred the tools and cradle there. On the way, he took the opportunity to absorb the surroundings.

Framed travel posters and mementos from other countries. Sleek, single-girl furniture. A hardwood floor with potted flowers strewn about. Naomi had commented once that she felt like the ultimate guest in Carissa's home and that she couldn't wait to have her own place someday. He sympathized with her, because sometimes he even felt the same way in his own damned apartment near Central Park. His real home had always been the office.

As if spurred by the discomfort of that notion, he unpacked the cradle. Soon, he recaptured the high of last night, when he'd helped Naomi in the store. The light labor had rushed through him, cleansing and even healing. For the first time in his life, he'd known that he could contribute with his own hands and efforts, not by buying flowers or jewels.

He could matter.

As he fixed the curved, supporting legs so that they stood upright, he even felt a measure of pride in what his work was producing. In fact, as he continued to throw himself so thoroughly into his labor, he didn't notice Naomi lingering near the doorway until he heard a sniffle.

David turned around, screwdriver poised, to find her wiping away a tear.

"It's beautiful," she said, sob-choked.

His heart fisted. He hadn't meant to make her cry, but these seemed like happy tears. Wasn't that a good thing?

"Hey," he said, "are you okay?"

She wandered closer. Then, running her fingers over the tiny, white little rosettes on the castings, she tenderly rocked the cradle, as if imagining Boo inside, waving his or her arms and gooing.

A strange tingle spiraled through his chest.

Then she started weeping again, softly, but it broke what he thought to be his heart all the same.

"Aw, Naomi," he said, trailing off because he wasn't sure how to handle this.

When he stood to go to her, she shook her head, as independent as ever. "Just look at me—a blubbering mess. It's these hormones, I think. I'm getting more tired and moody with every second."

"How about grabbing some rest then?" He reached out to take her arm, and she let him. "Just a catnap. You've got some time before *Flamingo Beach* comes on, and I'll be sure to wake you up."

Although she looked tempted, her stubborn streak seemed to win out, slashing across her gaze.

"The cradle," she said. "It was expensive, just like that dollhouse, wasn't it?"

David didn't want to lie to her, but he wasn't going to delve into details about "David," either. He was doing so well as "Dave," and to lose him seemed needless. Horrifying.

She wiped the remnants of her tears away, a determined slant to her expression. "What's really going on with you?"

At the threatening inquiry, he suddenly realized how damned comfortable he'd become as this downscale, old-jeans and new-attitude man. But it really was just a fantasy.

Or was it? Because Dave felt pretty real now. Telling her who he really was and how he was the complete opposite of the man she knew would destroy everything he'd worked so hard to earn.

It would destroy their mutually beneficial companionship, too.

Couldn't he just hold on for a little longer? Couldn't he keep making her happy by maintaining the status quo?

"Here," he said, leading her to the bed. "You might as well relax if we're going to talk."

He was buying time, his brain speeding a million different ways as he decided what he should do.

The right thing seemed to be to reveal the whole story, but resurrecting David truly wasn't right at all. His old self should stay buried, where he couldn't create any more trouble.

No doubt thinking that she was getting somewhere, Naomi went along with his request, climbing into bed, where she removed her slippers and tugged an afghan over her legs.

"More juice?" he asked, already halfway to the door.

"Dave—"

"Coming right up." He seized the chance to get away for a valuable moment.

As he poured her a glass of OJ in the kitchen, he forced himself to admit that Dave would *always* be honest, and retreating to a corner where he would debate with himself about coming clean wouldn't ever happen with a real man.

A pulse pounded in David's temple. Was this really all just a charade? Would he be able to stand strong as this new person once he stepped foot back in New York? If not, then he needed to give up Dave now.

No, he thought. God, no.

Yet, even while trying to maintain the warmth he'd discovered within himself, David knew that his stone coldness was still alive and well. He could feel the ice creeping into his bloodstream because that's what had always made him successful.

It's what had always protected him.

If he were smart, he would leave Placid Valley. Now, before Naomi got hurt. He would leave her with friendly memories of Dave, then make secretive arrangements for her to receive money so she and her child could live in comfort.

Necessary, he thought. This was the cleanest way to solve the situation: to have the stranger ride out of town before he brought more trouble.

Before he, himself, was destroyed.

That old pressure—the invisible weight that always

rode David—returned full force. It canted against his chest, his shoulders, as if embracing him after being banished.

David tried to deny it, picking up the glass of orange juice and making his way to Naomi's room.

When he entered, she was waiting, leaning forward, away from the pillows, her knees bent.

"Dave?" she asked. "Just tell me more, like you did last night. That's all I'm asking."

He could see the specters of Bill, of all the people who'd disappointed her in the past, shading her gaze.

Damn it, he wouldn't join their numbers. Not for anything.

Even a new chance at himself.

Giving her the juice, he smiled as Dave would— easy, casual, trustworthy Dave. "You want to know why I'm so free spending, do you?"

"I… Yes. Among other things."

Time to leave, the ice man thought. *She's getting too attached to a fantasy, and so are you.*

Fighting the coldness, he sat on the mattress. It sank under his bulk.

Okay, if you can't bring yourself to leave town now, then do what's necessary, Dave. *Tell her what she wants to hear and she'll never know better after you're gone. No harm, no foul.*

Out of desperation, he decided on this one little lie— the only way he could save them both.

"Lately," he said, "I came into some money. I gave myself time off from work, then decided to travel. That's all I'm about, Naomi. Simple as that."

The words tasted bitter, and he glanced away from

her, barely seeing how happy she was that he'd "revealed" more information.

Inside his chest, the ice hardened, a protective shield around his heart. But, when Naomi reached out and stroked his cheek, he melted quickly, violently.

Just as if Dave had finally made his own belated stand.

"See," Naomi said, "that wasn't so hard. I'm glad you told me."

She'd been dying to touch him while he worked on the baby bed. Watching him, her body had gone pliant as he'd put together the cradle, put together her life. His hard work and thoughtfulness had touched her on the most primal level. Even if she could have managed on her own, Dave was a provider. A real man who had been there for her during some recent low points.

Whether it was due to hormones or just plain lust, she was on fire. She knew what she wanted from Dave, and it went beyond the temporary convenience of having him around to help her out.

A rush of panic overcame her. Yes—Naomi the rebel, the independent, had gone and put her faith in another person besides herself. She'd accepted Dave's generosity, and that was saying something.

But what exactly *did* it say?

Why had she reacted this way to Dave and no one else?

As her fingertips traveled from his cheek to his mouth, he stopped her, holding her gently by the wrist. His gaze had gone a fevered blue, and she wasn't sure what was behind the clear emotion in them.

"You can't do that, Naomi," he said.

"What's stopping me?"

He closed his eyes, his jaw going tight. "Just...take my word on this, all right? You don't want to encourage me."

It was an invitation disguised as a rejection, she thought. Why?

"You said you didn't have a girlfriend or wife, God forbid." She slid her hand down to hold his. "I'm not sure what else could be holding you back."

Rough, warm skin... Oh, he felt nice.

Her hormones stirred like molecules bouncing off each other while boiling.

"I don't have any significant others," he said, voice ragged. "I never have."

But I could be significant, she thought, immediately brushing aside the sentiment. She didn't need that. Didn't want it. She was well on her way to feeling important on her own, after having moved out of a town that had beat her down with every passing day.

She inched closer to Dave. "Then why are you so determined to keep me at a distance?"

He paused, as if he didn't even know the answer himself.

"Dave, there's got to be a reason."

Finally, he looked her straight in the eye. It was as if he'd shot a laser of agony into her, all his emotions unleashed.

"I don't want to be the kind of man who takes advantage of you and then leaves, Naomi."

Desire flooded her, and it had nothing to do with lust. No, he cared, and it couldn't have been more obvious. She wasn't used to that on a purely intimate level.

In this moment of indecision, her body took over. She

leaned even closer to him. Close enough to take in his scent: clean, crisp, like the heady high of a new hundred-dollar bill.

"Listen, Dave," she whispered. "I know what I'm doing, what I need. You're going to be leaving soon, and I'm fine with that. *Very* fine, because I wouldn't be acting this way if you were going to stick around."

"Naomi…"

"I'm not asking you to go to bed with me." She laughed softly. "I made a mistake with Bill, and I've learned my lesson. It was too soon with him."

His gaze had gone bleary, and she closed the distance between them to a whisper.

"What are you asking for?" he said, choked.

It was heart-wrenchingly clear that he wouldn't deny her anything at this point. He'd given her so much, added so much to her life, that she didn't doubt he would fly her to the moon if she asked him to.

Tentatively, she rested her lips against the corner of his mouth, pressing a tiny kiss there, then speaking against his skin.

"I want to feel you against me. That's all. I'm not sure how far I should be going, anyway." She'd read that it was okay to go all the way, as long as she was comfortable. But she was wary about doing so.

Yet, truly, she just wanted to feel good, to have her blood racing around and pumping her full of happiness. There wasn't anything wrong with a fling, not as long as it stayed fleeting.

She touched another kiss on the other side of his mouth. His cheek scratched her lips, even though it was obvious he'd shaved this morning.

The thought of him scraping a blade over his skin— a man's task—sent delectable shivers over her. The sensation traveled inside of her, lower, until a buzz nestled between her legs.

"Dave?" she whispered, her mouth fully against his now.

She parted his lips with her tongue, and a jolt of desire rocked her. He groaned, as if in tortured protest, then gripped her upper arms as she angled forward, falling against him while he caught her.

Driven, she deepened the kiss, wrapping an arm around his shoulders and urging him on by pressing a hand to the back of his head. His hair was as thick as it was golden, something for her fingers to get lost in.

While she straddled him and sat on his lap, he seemed to snap, to give in to her wicked persuasions. He guided them both around so that he was sitting on the edge of the mattress, his palms traveling her back.

She clung to the image of those hands, so recently involved in the work of setting up the cradle, so willing to comfort her when she was sad. Knowing that they were memorizing her intimately elevated her passion, made her damp and ready for him.

As her breasts brushed his chest, she sucked in a breath.

He noticed, breaking off the kiss. "Are you…?"

"I'm all right," she panted, resting her forehead against his. "They're getting really sensitive."

She felt him starting to back away, but she put a stop to that quickly.

"No," she said. "Don't. Sensitive is good."

She liked how she was getting more voluptuous, was turned-on at the thought of sharing that with him.

So she guided his hand to her breast, watching how his eyes went unfocused. His undeniable passion screwed an ache through her, and she stifled a moan.

Slowly, he traced the new swells of her body, rubbed a finger around her nipple. Even through her T-shirt and bra, she enjoyed the exquisite pain from his touch.

A maelstrom built up inside her belly, stirring, making her shift on top of him. The pressure of her pants against the apex of her legs made her want to scream.

It was happening. One touch to such an innocent place and she was working her way to a climax already. Those had always been so hard for her to reach before, but now…

"Oh," she said, loving this feeling, loving…

No. She didn't love Dave. And she wouldn't make the mistake of talking herself into it just because he was making her crazy.

"Here," she said, reaching down to the hem of her shirt and jerking it up and over her head. She tossed the material away, then undid her bra.

As she sat before him, breasts bared and throbbing, she led both of his hands to them, eager and oblivious to everything but the starved look in his eyes. That, above all else, prodded her to another level.

Tenderly, he cupped her breasts, sketching his thumbs over the budding crests, making her bite her lip.

She wiggled on his lap, feeling his excitement, too. Taking advantage, she slid herself against the ridge of him, her core pounding, getting slicker by the moment.

When he lifted her and took a breast into his mouth, she cried out, her own arousal going tight and sharp, an ache that just got worse and better. He used his tongue expertly, bathing her, sucking until she couldn't stand it anymore.

Her mind and body seemed to explode into a swirl of colors, blending and merging like rainbows gone amok. The edges of each shade serrated her, drawing light from her skin, making her glow from a place inside that she hadn't discovered until now. She could feel that glow on her skin, too—she was damp with it, shattered and vibrating like a crimson bulb that had popped from too much heat.

At her cry of release, Dave laid her back on the mattress, his lips traveling down her stomach. He crouched over her, stopping at her belly, which he framed with his hands.

He placed a reverent kiss on the slight swell.

The baby, she thought. He hadn't forgotten, even in the midst of lovemaking.

She thought of her expanding waistline, but her orgasmic ride wouldn't allow her to care—not while he was worshipping her body.

Greedily, she worked at the buttons of her fly. He remained hovering over her, still unwilling to take advantage, as he'd put it.

"Don't worry," she said. "The underwear can stay on. We'll be good."

As she shucked off her capris, he got that dazed, hungry look in his eyes again, and she knew she'd won. That she'd taken Dave prisoner and wasn't letting him go.

She kicked the clothing to the mattress's edge, hearing it drop to the carpet. Outside her window, she could hear a plane humming by, cutting through a sky that was clear with gorgeous color and freedom.

"Take off your shirt," she said.

He obeyed her.

But after he pulled his shirt over his head, she saw that he was thinking too much again.

Intent upon persuading his body to make the decisions from here on out, she scanned his bare chest. He was fit, firm, his abs etched with muscles. She trailed her fingers over him, the ache gnawing between her legs once more.

Then she forgot herself—all the promises she had made to keep her head—and swept her fingertips over the bulge in his jeans.

He sucked in a breath, intercepting her progress by holding her hand away from him.

"Hey…" It was a warning.

"You're right," she said. "I know you're right."

Even her voice sounded distressed. Her body sure felt that way with having to hold back.

He seemed to recognize her restlessness, her need for another release.

With sweet deliberation, he kept eye contact with her while coasting his fingers between her legs, a tease.

She "ooh"ed slightly in surprise, then laughed, parting her thighs in acquiescence.

A dark, carnal smile lit over his mouth, and he slid his thumb between her folds. His touch was hard yet careful, reaching her most volatile pleasure point.

"There?" he said, pressing through the cotton of her panties.

"Oooooh…" She grabbed at the afghan, throttling it.

He had no mercy, taunting and circling until she moved her hips with his easy rhythm. Her breasts grew sore again, and she touched them out of a need to soothe herself, to keep from making too much noise.

But it didn't seem to work that way, because another harsh, wonderful roar was creeping up her body, consuming her in a wave of delight. It was like an aftershock—not as sudden as the first climax, but just as powerful.

He slid his other hand up her ribs, displacing her own palm as he cupped her breast. Her nipple got hard, so agonizingly sensitive that she thought she would burst right open.

Bit by bit, that wave crept higher, tugging an ocean of heat up and up. It licked at her with fluid flame, with white-hot insistence until she couldn't stave it off anymore.

Once again, an explosion ripped into her, as if the wave had crashed and pulped her into nothing.

In the aftermath of her sobbing cry, she realized that her body was arched, responding to his fingers in the only way it knew how.

Gasping for breath, she clutched at Dave, and he eased her down to the mattress, something else having taken the place of the hunger in his eyes.

But whatever it was, she lost sight of it when he sat up and held her against his chest, where she could feel his heartbeat flailing with as much uncertainty as her own.

Chapter Nine

After retreating to the restroom to get himself together, David returned to the bed, where he held Naomi close out of pure craving.

Pure guilt.

He'd created a hell by giving in to her, but when she'd come on so strong, he'd lost the struggle to refrain from taking advantage.

It'd been especially impossible when she had kept reminding him that their intimacies wouldn't be based on anything permanent, that she was *expecting* him to leave soon. She'd even sounded as if that was what she'd been hoping for.

So he'd given in, eager to give her what she wanted.

Except for the truth.

"You're one in a million, Naomi," he said, talking

near her ear. Her curls were still damp—from the shower and their activity.

She rested in the crook of his arm, nestled against his shoulder. "What do you mean by that? One in a million, I mean. Is that good or bad?"

"Good, very good. You're not like anyone I've ever known, and that's a fine thing."

"And…" She paused. "What kind of women have you known, Dave?"

He glued his thoughts together for a moment. "All business. As warm as a guttered streetlamp after you've been just about as intimate with another person as you can get…at least physically."

Naomi placed a hand over his bare stomach, and his muscles flinched at her soft touch. Whether she knew it or not, she'd imprinted him, and right here, right now, he was hers.

All hers.

When she spoke, her words were warm against his shoulder. "Are you saying that you dated women who only wanted you for your bod?"

"That's one way of putting it. And I never minded that. It fit into my schedule. Relationships are work and, unless you want to invest your time in one, they fall to low priority on the list of life."

"That's…" She scribbled her fingers over his skin while trying to come up with a decent description.

He helped her out. "That's sad. I know. I've heard it enough times to realize it."

Especially from his father.

And from his own conscience.

"But," he said, toying with Naomi's hair, "I didn't

mind my lifestyle. Not until my brother got married and had kids. I never thought something like my nephew getting excited when I came through the door for dinner or my niece giving me a hug for no reason whatsoever would matter. But it does."

As silence cushioned them, David realized something. Maybe his dad's expectations for him to find that perfect family had only been an excuse for David to finally leave and seek a change. He hadn't wanted to admit, even in the throes of a life crisis, that there could be something more profoundly disturbing going on inside of him.

A genuine longing for love and a family of his own.

He nestled his fingertips against Naomi's tummy, where Boo was waiting to be born. This very moment, while holding Naomi and her child, David knew peace.

Naomi slid her hand to the other side of him, hugging him to her as if not wanting to let him go. And he didn't want to leave. He wanted everything to crystallize and remain the same as it was now, while the apartment's walls creaked and the birds outside called to each other.

"Tell me some details about your romantic past," Naomi said. "I know you haven't been real serious about anyone, but isn't there some kind of story about the most important relationship you've ever had?"

"No. No stories."

"Really?"

"I'm not…lying." He swallowed. Funny how he couldn't bring himself to fib about anything but the most important aspect of himself. "I've never committed to much besides a business contract."

"I thought you might've been exaggerating."

"No." The more he talked about it, the more acutely embarrassed he became.

The ice man.

But wasn't deserting that personality a start? Dave should be proud of the accomplishment, in fact, but for this lie keeping an invisible distance between him and this warm, loving woman.

"I'm not judging you for your past, Dave," she said, her lips coming to rest against his skin, "I told you that I've been with two men my whole life, and neither of them worked out. I'm not exactly Queen Expert of Wonderful Relationships."

He ran a finger down her arm, watching the fine hairs stand on the end of emerging goose bumps. She wriggled closer against him, her mouth forming a smile on his flesh.

"I thought you were a rebel in the good old days, Naomi. A total of two conquests does not a bad girl make."

"I was all bark and no bite. Besides Bill, there was senior year, prom night, a cliché in its most disheartening form."

A prom. David had gone to prep school, and he'd been so involved in final exams and projects that he'd skipped dances and end-of-school parties altogether.

"Who was your date?" he asked.

"Sean Canady. I'd nursed a crush on him since I was a freshman, so when he asked me, I was beside myself. I went to Lexington with my friends and bought a decent dress with some pin money I'd raised on the weekends, working at the grocery store."

"I'll bet you looked pretty, in a very goth way, of course."

She laughed, once again infusing him with the desire to explore her, to bring her against him and feel every curve mold to his body. To be inside of her.

"I did wear a black dress," she said. "And lots of eye makeup. A Very Special Kiss-My-Grits prom—that's what I was going for."

"And it turned out to be a flop?"

"It did. Not that my every Sean Canady dream didn't come true that night, but—" a brittle laugh "—he took me out for an elegant dinner beforehand and we danced every dance, then we went to an after-party, where I decided he was deserving of my virginity. That part wasn't disappointing at all. It was only the days afterward, when I thought he might appreciate what I'd given him a tad more, that I vowed to be more careful with everyone I met in the future."

Remorse speared him again, so he held her closer, telegraphing that he was sorry. So damned sorry.

"If you didn't have sex with anyone before prom night," he said, "I'd guess that you were already being careful."

"Oh, I teased the boys, don't get me wrong about that. There was some power in getting them going and then putting a stop to it. I'm not proud of admitting this, but it's true. And since I was such 'trash,' everyone said that I was doing the big deed with those boys anyway. It gave me a perverse pleasure to know the tongue waggers were wrong—that I was better than what they were saying. I just wished I could prove it once and for all."

"And that's what you're doing right now. Proving all of them wrong by raising Boo to the best of your abilities."

He wondered what Naomi would think if she only knew that she was revealing her "trashy" history to

David Chandler—billionaire and former snob—and not to a regular Dave who'd recently come into some money. She would be mortified, no matter how many times he tried to tell her that he *didn't* think any less of her. As a matter of fact, she probably wouldn't ever believe that he had put her on a pedestal of sorts, that he admired her strength and determination.

She propped herself on her elbows, and the motion skimmed her breasts over his chest. At the sound of her sharp inhalation, and at the sight of her nipples beading, his skin hummed.

"I keep thinking," she said, "that the people in Kane's Crossing will someday see that I'm a better mother than any of my foster moms were, that I would've been a stand-up woman who never needed any of them anyway. I know it's all a dream, because most of them would never forget I had a child out of wedlock, but I can't erase that hope. I just can't."

He wanted to ask her what would happen to her dream if someone stepped in to help her with supermom duty. If she would still think herself so wonderful and heroic if she didn't do it all on her own.

However, he also wondered if she truly didn't have a need for him beyond what he could supply monetarily. Sure, she had appreciated his presence at the ultrasound appointment, but he'd just been a grace note. She would've done fine on her own, if it came down to it.

Right?

He recalled the look on her face after the doctor's visit, the gratefulness and…something more?

Did she need him, after all?

"Are you ever going back to Kane's Crossing?" he asked, his throat tight. He wished she would need him.

With a pause, she seemed to turn that over in her mind. The tilt of her head, the darkness of her gaze told him that it wasn't an easy call.

"Maybe someday," she finally said, sinking back down to rest her head against him again. "We all have to go home at a certain point, after all. Don't we?"

It wasn't a rhetorical question. She was asking *him*.

But he didn't have an answer. Not anymore.

An hour later, Dave had persuaded Naomi to go ahead down the block to The Suds Club to watch her soap with the others. He said that he wanted to put the finishing touches on the cradle and promised he would be waiting for her when she got back.

Based on what he'd told her about never committing, she was stunned that he would be sticking around. She even wondered if Dave didn't normally cuddle up with his paramours after getting his physical satisfaction with them, but maybe she was making a mountain out of a molehill.

At any rate, she was pleased, yet shaken all the same, that he would be there. It seemed symbolic in some way, as if they'd reached a turning point in their confusing relationship.

If that was what you could call what they had...

When Naomi entered the Laundromat, she found it mainly empty, except for two sporadic watchers and Liam McCree in his regular corner tapping away at his computer.

Since she had a few minutes until the soap started, she stopped to say hi to him.

"Where's your sidekick?" he asked, putting the lid of his computer down and devoting all his attention to her.

"Dave? He's not exactly a...sidekick."

Liam gave her a roguish smile, understanding completely. He had a slight goatee, and that, coupled with his dark, two-weeks-past-a-decent-cut hair, made him come off as a scamp. That's what Jenny always said, anyway.

"What's got you smiling like a canary-eating tomcat?" Naomi asked, wanting to talk about Dave and... not wanting to.

Yeesh, he had her mightily puzzled.

"What exactly is Dave to you?" he asked, cocking an eyebrow.

"A friend." There—a nicely packaged word that could encompass most anything.

"A friend with benefits?" Liam said wryly.

As Naomi stood there with her mouth agape, he elaborated.

"Oh, Naomi, Naomi. You've got—" he motioned to his face, then hers "—that thing going on."

A glow? A dumb post-foolin'-around grin?

She held a hand to her cheek as Liam continued.

"It kind of reminds me of what a person looks like when they jog around the block a few times. You look...satisfied. And I'm pretty sure you weren't out jogging, either."

"Aren't you the perceptive one?"

"I'm a keen observer of human nature, that's all."

Naomi wondered just how much Liam did absorb, sitting here in the corner by himself almost every day. All they really knew about him was that he and Jenny had regular spats for no good reason.

Naomi just construed that as inept flirting, though.

She held her hand up in a farewell, but Liam stopped her with his next words.

"You ever ask your Dave about why he's so interested in babies?"

Naomi turned to Liam.

"Mei and Jenny might've mentioned that to me," he added. "Usually the whole baby issue is enough to make a guy run the other way with his hair on fire."

He'd brought up a good question, one that had been haunting the back of her mind, but she'd avoided it. Still, Liam's addressing it rankled her, mainly because she'd wanted to ask Dave more about it and she hadn't.

She'd had other questions on her mind. A legion of them.

"Just because you're afraid of babies doesn't mean other men are," she said. "Not everyone is a free spirit like you."

"Hey." Liam held up his hands, caught. "I am what I am. Don't get on me because I'm asking about Dave and you can't answer."

"Maybe," she said, "Dave is at the point in his life when he wants kids. Maybe he's drawn to me because of that."

"Maybe?" Now Liam leaned forward, his expression going from canary-eating to a more serious, concerned one. "I sure wish you knew more about him than *maybe,* Naomi."

Unsettled, she resumed her way toward the TV, where the soap had already started. In the background, she heard Liam laboring away on his keyboard again, amidst the thumping of dryers and washers.

All through her program, the questions kept tapping at her, too, goading her to get answers before she gave her heart to a man she still didn't know very well.

If she hadn't given her heart away already.

David had about an hour to put the final touches on the cradle, including the bedding. When he finished, he went to the market, knowing Naomi had the night off and wishing to do everything he could for her.

Maybe he was just buttering her up, in case he found the courage to tell her everything about himself tonight. Or maybe this would be a goodbye dinner.

He only thought that because he'd been ambushed by a cell phone call from Lucas, who had arranged a conference connection with Gabriel, David's nephew. Yup, Lucas was pulling out the big guns in order to sway his brother to come back to New York.

And he had almost done the job, too.

But what would Lucas think if he knew that David had found something like a possible family here?

A month ago, he would've wanted his sibling to feel threatened because David was now on a level playing field with their father again.

But…no. Not anymore. He was actually fantasizing about introducing Naomi to the clan, anticipating their enthusiasm.

It would be the first time he had truly come home, with her by his side.

Knowing he was acting like a besotted fool, he put together the makings of pasta and a salad—it was the only thing he knew how to cook on the fly, without his house staff around. Meanwhile, he went over his options with Naomi again and again, getting more bewildered with every go-round.

Even so, when she came back to the apartment, he'd prepared the small dinner table near the common area with flowered plates and linen napkins, some candles lit and wavering in a near-evening breeze from an open window.

Naomi had her head down as she entered, and he caught a fleeting hint of sorrow as she raised her gaze. It slayed him.

But when she saw the table, she brightened, the candlelight reflected in her eyes.

"What did you do here?" she asked.

"I made your night off an easy one." He pulled out a chair for her. "It's nothing fancy, but I tried my best. Hope you don't mind spaghetti sauce from a jar."

"I adore Italian food, any way it comes."

"I made sure the sauce had healthy ingredients. And there's salad and fresh-baked bread, as well. Then fruit for dessert—but be warned. I got it from the market's deli, so I can't take credit for it."

"Stop, it all sounds wonderful."

She took a seat, an emotion so soul-bruising, so confused, in her gaze that he had to avert his own. With care, he placed the napkin over her lap, then served the meal.

Once he was settled, too, they dug in.

"This is the bee's knees," she said, smiling slightly as she bit into her parmesan-sprinkled bread.

But he could tell there was something behind her smile—something uneasy and lingering.

"Bee's knees?" he asked, fearful of the moment she

would lose her forced lightheartedness. "I think that's something one of my grandmas would've said."

Slowly, she set down the bread, and he knew the moment had come.

Tell her, he thought. *She deserves to know who you really are and what you've become because of her. Tell. Her.*

"Dave," she said, "you've done so much for me, and I'm thankful for every bit of it."

"But?" he said, helping her along, feeling as if he were being led from a cell of his own choosing to a raised dais where he would be put out of his misery with bladed words.

And now that it was happening, he felt relieved.

"But," she repeated, "I've got a lot more questions, and maybe I have no right to the answers, with you going back home soon and all. Still, I wish I knew you better. I wish…"

What? he wondered. Did she wish he *would* stick around?

He doubted it. Getting people angry at him was par for the course in his life, and he was about to repeat that pattern now, even if all he'd tried to do was avoid it.

The ice man returns, he thought, heart sinking. He was what he was, and redemption wouldn't dismiss his past.

He took a deep breath, then had at it.

"Naomi, I've done some bad things over the years. I've manipulated others and generally worked them over so many times I've stopped keeping count. I would eat the people around me for breakfast, lunch and dinner."

She'd gone quiet, the candlelight flickering between them, the sounds of infrequent traffic from the street motoring by, reminding him that he could leave right now if he decided to.

He clenched his fingers on his knees, staying.

"Yet something happened to change all that. I went too far with a business deal. I designed a plan that involved my brother, and it required him to marry a sweet woman who would erase his bad reputation. He was a playboy, and that wasn't good for business, especially since we wanted to acquire a family-oriented company that didn't look fondly upon Lucas's…activities."

By now, Naomi had leaned back in her chair, face blank.

He forged on. Too late to stop. "I even convinced him to adopt a son, so they would be a 'real' family. And he did it, all without being aware that I had other things on the agenda, such as using her ethnicity to appeal to a customer base."

Naomi's forehead furrowed. "*You* did this?"

Her question struck home. Had he really changed so much that she couldn't see he was capable of such dirty deeds?

He felt ill. "I did that, Naomi, and all I want is to make up for it." His fingernails were cutting into his palms. "Lucas fell for Alicia, and he became a great husband and father. And to see the look on my dad's face when Lucas turned his life around… It was a revelation. He'd never respected Lucas before and now my brother is the one who makes him proud. My brother, the screwup. That left me behind in a very personal way, and all I've wanted is to get my dad's affection and respect back. I have no idea how to function being 'the other son.'"

"So you went in search of a family, just like your brother had?"

He could see so clearly that he had already betrayed her, even without the billionaire news. She looked darkened, like a room where the lights have been doused.

"I'm sorry," he started, wanting to tell her more.

But she wasn't having it. "Are you saying you planned to bring me back to your home to show me off and make yourself feel better?"

"No, I'm trying to tell you that you mean the…"

…*world to me.*

She'd risen from her chair with great dignity. She wasn't crying—maybe because she was too shocked that yet another person in her life had crept up behind her to give her a shove into a brick wall.

"I need you to leave, Dave."

At her words, panic slammed him. All his worst fears, all his hopes… He wanted to grab for them, save them.

He stood. "Naomi, there's a lot more I need to tell you."

"I don't want to hear it. Just…leave."

The last word cracked and, as if to repair the damage, she went to the door and opened it, looking away from him.

Truthfully, if he were Naomi, he wouldn't be able to stand seeing him, either. He doubted he would even be able to go back to his hotel and look in the mirror without smashing it to bits.

Respecting her wishes, he made the longest walk ever to the door, his world crumbling with each step. But he had to say one last thing.

"I was only trying to create a clean slate for myself,

Naomi. And I found it to be so easy whenever I was with you."

She averted her face even more, maybe to hide the destruction he'd visited on her. That was the hardest part of all—her rejection of the best man he could put forward.

With a last glance, he walked out of her apartment because that's what she wanted.

David went down in the elevator, almost bumping into another man on his way up as he all but stumbled out.

All the while, the ice returned, protecting what was left of him, inching through his veins and upward, stiffening his posture into that of a man who looked as if he owned everything around him.

Even though he had nothing.

When Naomi shut the door behind Dave, she forced herself to keep it closed.

She wouldn't cry. No, never, not anymore.

Crying would've meant that she'd expected more out of a person. Crying would've shown that she'd started to care about Dave too much, and she hadn't allowed herself to get that far.

Wasn't that true? He'd merely been a fling, and that's what she had wanted. She'd been the one to control the progress of their relations, and that felt good. She had even been the one to end things. She had obviously disappointed *him* this time instead of the other way around.

At least, that's what she kept telling herself as she kept her hands on the door.

Everything he'd revealed kept flying around her mind; she couldn't get a handle on any of it.

A business acquisition…his brother and his wife and a child…manipulations…

The Dave she knew couldn't have done any of that. But when she thought of the man she'd met that first day in the Laundromat—the stiff admiral of a man—she realized that she'd been far too trusting once again. Even after she'd promised herself to be on guard.

Still…

She thought of Dave watching the ultrasound monitor. Dave working so hard to put together that cradle. Dave kissing her, caressing her…

A knock on the door shuddered her to attention. It was loud, purposeful, and without thinking, she impulsively went to open it.

But when the doorway revealed a man dressed in a faded suit, Naomi wanted to slam him out of her sight.

Just as she'd done before.

"Wait, Naomi, please," Bill Vassey said, holding the door open. "We've got to talk."

Chapter Ten

"Naomi, I've come a long way to see you," Bill said. "So don't shut me out again."

Fear tore through her, but all she could do was stand there, unable to move. Unable to run away as she had done before.

He'd found her, and the father of her child would try to use his salesman silver-tongue to get what he wanted, too. But she would never, ever give up her baby. She had already told him that, so why had he come all the way across the country to hear it again?

Hands shaking, she held her ground, grabbing onto the door to keep herself standing upright. "I know you're here to tie up your loose ends, Bill, but I've already knotted all mine."

"I can't believe you left, not when we needed to work so much out. It didn't take a lot of effort to learn that you were with your friend Carissa. Her sister gave me the address because she knew this was urgent."

"Urgent? When she finds out you stretched the truth, she's not going to be happy."

"I told you I'd be back to talk, Naomi."

"And I told you I'd be gone."

They faced off, at an impasse. Why hadn't Bill shown up just minutes earlier, when Dave was here? Although she could handle this, it was always nice to have backup....

Dave.

His name sent a pang of longing through her.

As her heart wrung itself out, Naomi blocked her so-called friend out of her mind. She still couldn't grasp what he'd done—trying to use her and her baby for his own needs.

Don't think about it.

Instead, she focused on how Bill's black hair was nicely combed, his suit pressed. He had always tried hard to seem well put together and it was only now that Naomi noticed a thread or two hanging off his jacket.

"I won't stay long," he finally said. "And I don't want to bother your neighbors by standing in the hallway during this discussion."

Obviously, he wasn't going to be put off. And she couldn't run away from this, not with him so determined.

Yet she could still maintain control.

"Five minutes," she said, "that's all you have."

When he agreed, she thought of how odd this had turned out: Bill was getting more of a chance than she'd given Dave tonight....

Dang it all, why hadn't she let him explain more before she'd asked him to leave? Had she used a judgmental shield to cut herself off from hearing everything he had to say for fear that it would be even more hurtful than what she'd *already* heard from him?

Maybe it was the distance she already felt from Bill that allowed her to numbly open the door to him. He couldn't hurt her anymore, not the way Dave had.

Still, she kept that door gaping after her ex entered.

He went to the dinner table, where the food was going to waste. Most of the candles had been snuffed out by a breeze that had started to blow harder and colder from the window.

"So," she said, wanting to get this over and done with, "what needs to be clarified, Bill? Are you here to make that appointment for me to 'get rid' of my baby?"

"You make it sound so harsh."

Maybe she was mistaken, but there was a weariness in his dark eyes.

"As I recall," she said, trying to stay calm, "you talked about 'taking care of the problem,' and then you left on your all-important client trip, ignoring everything I said about how much I wanted to keep our child. You laid down your law and I laid down mine."

"And I still feel the same way, but there's a reason for it. One I never got to explain. You should've waited for a more opportune time for us to talk, not when I was running to the airport. You know how significant my trip was."

Absently, she had come to splay her hands against her belly, against Boo, as if she could block out this conversation from her baby's hearing.

"There was no conceivable reason worth waiting for." Naomi rubbed at the slight curve beneath her palms.

"You were horrified at my news, and that told me everything I needed to know about how you felt. Period."

"No, you don't know the half of it, Naomi."

He wasn't comprehending her side of the story, as usual, so she tried to make him see where she was coming from.

"I had my first ultrasound, Bill, and I saw my baby. He or she has a heart that's beating, just the same as either of ours. How can you be so callous about that?"

She imagined the moment she'd first seen Boo. Imagined the adoration on Dave's face while he'd looked at her baby.

Bill didn't have nearly the same expression as he faced her now.

"I told you," he said quietly, "no kids. I couldn't have been clearer about it. And, believe me, I beat myself up over the fact that we should've used more than a condom."

"I was just as careless, but I don't understand why you'd care. I left town to raise this child on my own, and I'm not asking you for any kind of support, now or in the future."

"I'm sorry, but I can't depend on that." He flinched, as if recognizing how hard he sounded.

Naomi kept sheltering her belly. "What're you saying? Do you think I'm going to come back one day and demand that you play daddy? Well, I can vow that's not going to happen."

Not even if she were destitute.

"You say that now." Bill ran a hand through his dark hair, messing it up from its carefully combed style. "But, believe me, things change. I know this firsthand, and that's what I'm concerned about."

She girded herself, sensing bad news coming.

He rested a hand on the back of a chair, his knuckles pale with the strain. "Back in Illinois, I've got an ex-girlfriend. And...a son, too."

Silence, as he waited for her to react.

Not...comprehending...

There were too many truths hitting her tonight, first with Dave, now Bill.

"You never told me," she said, the words barely coming out.

"She's out of my life." Bill's gaze went hazy. "My high school girlfriend. She got pregnant during the summer after graduation, and I never even knew. See, I went off to college out of state, and she stayed home. We drifted apart and when I came back to town, she had moved. Then she ended up getting married, and I didn't hear from her again until years later, after her divorce. She was asking me for child support payments. And after a DNA test and a battery of legal crap, she's getting them."

Blindsided...making no sense...

"You think I'm going to be the same way?" Naomi asked.

"There's no guarantee that you won't be, and I'm not equipped to handle another child. Damn, I can't even handle one." By now, Bill seemed to lack any fight whatsoever. "No matter what you say now about doing this on your own, there's no guarantee that you're not going to end up asking me to step in. A child needs so much and, unfortunately, I'm not up to raising one. I already knew that, and I warned you."

"So you want me to erase *my* child because he or she might be inconvenient for you in the future."

Bill's cheeks grew red. "I never asked for this responsibility."

"You had sex with me, Bill. Isn't that the same as asking?"

Disgust—with herself most of all—coated Naomi. You play, you pay, right? Why hadn't she listened to his warnings and abstained from making love with him because of that? Had she been so damned needy for affection?

She only wished Bill were a different type of man, one who had the potential to be a good father to her child. But the only one she knew on a deeper level had already walked out her door because she had asked him to.

Stupid, she thought. *I've got to be stupid.*

"You know, Bill," she added in the silence, "maybe you ought to get a vasectomy if this is such an issue for you."

"Maybe you're right."

His response startled her because the last thing she'd been expecting was for him to admit to his faults. He seemed beaten, and that got to her, because she knew what it was like to withstand the punches life threw.

But she also knew that both she and Bill had brought the fight on themselves through their own actions.

The realization turned her stomach. She invited trouble, that's all there was to it. She must've been a magnet, a born loser.

"Why didn't you tell me before about your girlfriend and your son?" she asked, needing to know how she could prevent getting herself into these corners in the future.

With Bill.

With Dave.

Bill gripped the chair harder. "I suppose I thought our relationship was still too new. I didn't want you to leave me when you heard, because I knew that would be your first instinct. It's happened to me before in relationships, so I've learned to wait. I wanted to be sure you cared for me enough to understand."

"You didn't think I held enough affection for you to take the news well?"

He finally met her stare. "No. You can be kind, and you've got a good heart. But you do have a judgmental streak about a mile long, Naomi."

His comment felt like a slap, but she knew what he said was true. And her distrustfulness and intolerance had reared its full power on Dave tonight, hadn't it?

But that judgmental streak was the only thing keeping her safe. It told her to run when a situation was dangerous. It wrapped her up in caution, like the womb of a loving mother she never had.

"That's still no excuse for keeping the truth from me," she said, finding that even though Bill was in the room, she was actually talking to Dave, wishing he were around for her to be saying this to him in person.

Wishing he would understand why she had kicked him out.

"Once again, Naomi, you're right." Bill looked at her closely. "I had no excuse."

His scrutiny made her realize that she was on the edge of crying, so she took control of herself.

"Maybe we should take this up tomorrow," he added.

"No." She shook her head, using the back of her hand to wipe away the tears before they fell. "You're not going to talk me into anything. Go home and carry on. I won't be back. I won't ever even contact you."

"Naomi…"

His tone indicated that he hadn't given up his cause yet, and that threatened her.

But Bill wouldn't have any sway. Boo was the only person who truly belonged to her now and, more than ever, Naomi was determined never to lose her baby.

Even if she'd already lost so much tonight.

Just as she was about to tell Bill to get out for good, a voice interrupted from the doorway, and Naomi's heart seemed to flare open at the sound of it.

"You heard her," Dave said, gaze drilling Bill. "Now get out before I escort you myself."

David hadn't even made it out the lobby's exit before he had stopped himself.

One step out that door, he'd thought, and it was over. The ice was already consuming him, and all that had been keeping it at bay was Naomi.

Should he brave the risk of returning to her?

David didn't know for sure, even as he found himself riding the elevator back up. All the same, he sure as hell knew he couldn't take another vacation from what was happening to him right now.

To *them*—him and Naomi and Boo.

As he approached Naomi's door, preparing himself to withstand her possible anger at his return, he saw that it was open. Then he heard voices—hers and…a man's.

Warily, David lingered outside, listening for a moment, realizing who her visitor was.

Boo's father.

It felt as if a board had taken David out at the knees, but he stayed standing, leaning his back and head against the far wall.

As the conversation wore on and he learned much more than he should've known, David thought that maybe he *should* get going. Then again, he didn't want to leave Naomi alone with the man she'd run from in the first place. She had kept her door open for a reason, maybe because it felt safer that way.

Yes, he would be here in case she needed him.

But the point came when it sounded as if Naomi was prematurely ending the conversation, and Bill was reluctant to depart.

David tried not to feel the sting of Naomi tossing *him* out earlier. He also tried not to be bothered by her habit of not giving another person an opportunity to fully explain their side of the story, just as she might've done with Bill when she left Kane's Crossing.

But that wasn't a priority right now, so David moved to the doorway and told Bill to get out.

In the aftermath of his ultimatum, David could feel Naomi's gaze on him, so he met her eyes. Was that relief…or happiness…to see him?

Was there something else there, too? A banked glow, a mockery of the light that had always greeted him in those olive eyes.

Damn him for what his lying had done to her.

Bill, a fellow businessman, had crossed his arms over his chest at David's sudden appearance. Did Naomi's ex recognize him from esoteric industry articles about "the Chandler Brain"?

As David held his breath at the answer, Bill seemed

to discard the subject, as if wanting to still think about it before actually asking.

"Are you the apartment manager or something?" the ex inquired cautiously instead.

Naomi broke in at that point. "He's a friend, and he's also asking you to go."

A friend. At least David was still that.

Wasn't he?

"All right," Bill said, holding up his hands, "I'm on my way."

David stepped inside a few more feet, clearing the exit for the other man.

Bristling, he inspected the approaching Bill Vassey. So this was Boo's biological father—a man in an exhausted suit that tried too hard to impress. A guy who had kept certain truths from Naomi, too.

The closer he got, the more David related.

Bill looked over his shoulder as he reached the threshold. "Naomi, I'll be at a motel just around the block. The Clairemont, on Lily Vale Lane."

With her arms wrapped over her belly, Naomi seemed too worn-out to acknowledge her ex. Or perhaps she was finished arguing for the night. Circles darkened the skin beneath her eyes, and all David wanted to do was lay her down, then watch her fall into a serene sleep. This drama couldn't be healthy for Boo, either.

"Don't expect a social call," David said, grabbing the doorknob and getting ready to close Bill out. If Naomi wouldn't cap this off, he sure as hell would.

The other man paused, then tacked on one final comment to his ex-girlfriend. "Just know that I would take care of any cost involved with a...procedure."

David froze. But before he could lay into Bill, Naomi came to life, eyes blazing with the fire of a mother protecting her child.

"If you had seen this baby, how beautiful he or she already is, with those little limbs, that tiny body, you wouldn't ever mention a 'procedure' again."

Something like shame seemed to escort Bill the rest of the way out. At least, that's what David read in the man's eyes.

Even stone-cold David had been overcome that day when he'd looked at Boo, but *he* had fallen for the child without reservation.

Just as he had fallen for the mom, too.

"If you'd been at that ultrasound," David said through gritted teeth, "you'd think again about what you're suggesting."

Bill paused in his leaving, glancing at David one last time, a glint of near recognition in his eyes. It seemed to intensify, then disappear again.

Just go, David thought. *Before everything gets worse.*

"So your friend was at the ultrasound?" Bill asked Naomi. "Good friend."

"Yes," she said, voice breaking, "he…is."

When she glanced at David, her eyes held the shards of her shattered trust in him, but there was another quality among the splinters.

Affection?

Or an emotion even stronger than that?

Blades of confusion sliced through him. Even if she'd told him to leave, did she still care?

Then it happened.

Bill raised a finger, pointing at David. "You know, I

think I recognize you. It took me a minute or two, but I'm pretty sure."

No, David thought. *Not when there's a chance that Naomi might tolerate having me in the same room again.*

"Hell, Naomi," Bill said, "you traded up, didn't you?"

The guy had donned a smile that told David he was trying to poke at Naomi with this comment. Now, David could see why she had left, if the man had hidden a worse side for so long and only revealed it the night she'd told him she was pregnant.

"What are you talking ab—?" Naomi started asking.

"TCO, The Chandler Corporation," Bill rushed on. "David Chandler, the tycoon. Under any other circumstances, I'd be glad to meet you, Mr. Chandler."

But David was watching Naomi, having withstood the inevitable. Ready for its aftermath.

"I tried to tell you," he said softly.

Her face was turning a bright red, and he knew it was probably because she was remembering all the "trash" stories she'd told to a man she thought was so much like her—except suddenly fatter in the pockets because of a windfall. He wished Bill wasn't here so he could assure her that none of her embarrassing stories had tainted her.

She looked down at the floor. "I didn't trade up, *Bill.* You know better than that."

"Did I hear you right?" Bill asked. "David Chandler never got around to telling you who he was?"

She heaved in a sharp breath, and it pierced David's world. He knew she must be deflating inside: her pride, the trust she'd put into him when she'd asked why he had so much money to be throwing around and he'd answered with a lie.

"Get out of here, Mr. Vassey," David said, all serious business.

Bill laughed, shaking his head as he walked down the hallway, repeating, "She didn't know," to himself with amusement.

But even as David closed the door, he couldn't help feeling as if there hadn't been any closure. Not between Naomi and Bill and not between him and this woman, either.

They didn't say anything for a moment as David lingered at the door. He didn't know if he should be leaving or staying.

"You must think I'm quite the hick," she said, barely above a whisper.

"No, I don't."

"You don't have to pretend it's any other way, Dave. Or...David."

She was obviously in shock at hearing who he was, and he could tell her mind was spinning at full speed to understand what he was doing in her apartment. At the same time, all her defenses were up and operational. He'd expected this: disgrace from a woman who'd fought all her life to be better than anyone ever gave her credit for.

She continued. "You heard everything before you came in then, Mr. Chandler?"

"Don't Mr. Chandler me, Naomi. And, yes, I heard everything, but I still think you're the most amazing woman I've ever met."

"How can you say that?" She hugged herself tighter. "How many women do you know who'd be dumb enough to get themselves into a relationship with a man who got another woman pregnant…a man who's paying child support and doesn't want to be a father? And then she sleeps with that man and expects him to be happy at the news of a child after he's told her he doesn't want any?"

"You can't get angry at yourself for not knowing what he was up to."

"But I should've been on my toes and looked for signals—like the phone calls he would make when he thought I wasn't around, and then when he saw that I was, pretend that it was his mom or aunt or something. I should've opened my eyes."

David knew they weren't just talking about Bill. She was flagellating herself for his own lie.

"I know," he said, "that Bill had an excuse for not telling you about his past. I have one, too, and I really did believe I was doing the right thing. I thought I'd be gone by now, and that we'd never be close enough for my identity to matter. I didn't set out to hurt you—not like I set up Lucas to hurt his wife. I truly wanted to be Dave and forget about David."

"But David is a billionaire, isn't he? He's not the man I know at all."

She'd given up on him—he could see that in the slump of her shoulders. Worst of all, it seemed she'd retreated behind her walls and she wasn't ever going to come out. *He* had done that to her.

"I have no idea who I am anymore," he said, heat gathering in his throat and making it hard to talk.

"Well, you'll know when you get back to your job after vacation."

David cleared his throat, hating the weakness, then wishing he could embrace it, because it *wasn't* a weakness.

It was human. Clearly far beyond his capabilities, after all.

He made one last bid to hold on. "But...what if I stayed, Naomi? Who would I be then?"

Such shock overtook her that he actually stepped back. Then he realized she was...terrified.

Terrified of the moment when he would inevitably wound her again, just as she believed all people would. And he'd done a damned good job of proving that.

He couldn't stand to see her this way and, instinctively, the ice attacked him. It prevented him from reaching out to her, from causing any more trouble than he already had.

Maybe David wouldn't be such a monster anymore—those days were gone—but that didn't mean the ice couldn't be used to keep him from wreaking more damage on her.

He knew that now.

All that was left to do was help her recover in any way he could, because he obviously couldn't manage anything else. At the very least, he needed to make sure no one would ever get to her and Boo.

If he could leave her with that, maybe she could forgive him some day.

"If there's anything I can do to make this up to you, Naomi," he said, "tell me."

"Make it up?" Naomi's lower lip trembled before she bit down on it. How could they possibly go anywhere from here? "We've both been making things up all along, haven't we? You made up another life, and I made up a fantasy about how I fit into that life. It's time to face reality, David."

Then, putting an end to the discussion, she started walking to her room, where she could enclose herself in another type of womb. She felt numb enough to need it, as if floating in thick liquid that blinded her.

David Chandler was a wealthy, wealthy man. Her tiny imagination hadn't even approached such a possibility.

God, he must think she was truly trash. All those stories she'd told him, all the neurotic hang-ups she'd laid bare. He would probably laugh about them at the next cocktail party.

Surely that's all she'd been to him—a story to tell. Because what else would a man like him want with a bumpkin like her?

"Naomi," he said.

The pain in his voice urged her to face David. At the sight of him, she felt pulled, magnetized toward something so innately right, yet intellectually wrong. Attraction didn't mean a darn thing if she couldn't trust who he was.

Even so, for a second, she wanted to run to him, to throw herself into his arms.

But she didn't.

He noticed her choice, nodding as if having to agree with her. That ached most of all—seeing this strong man bruised because she needed to protect herself and her child.

"Just know," he said, "that I would do anything for you and Boo. Anything. So don't you worry about Bill, okay? You just rest easy."

Though his words were heated, his tone was frosty, unfamiliar. For the first time since he'd come into the Laundromat, she saw the powerful billionaire, and she couldn't reconcile herself with that.

How could she when he had so much to give and she didn't?

Just as she was about to ask him what he meant by doing "anything" for her, he crisply turned around and headed out the door.

Naomi touched her tummy again, wanting to go after him, but knowing it was best that she stayed away.

David Chandler was back, and he was on a mission.

As he drove the short distance to Bill's motel on Lily Vale Lane, streetlights whisked by in frozen streaks. He knew now that Naomi would never forget what he'd done to her, and that was something he couldn't live with, no matter how much he longed to try.

Meanwhile, he'd constructed elements of Dave into the old, frigid framework, snapping a do-gooder spine into the place of the greedy one. A mixture of both men, because that's what he needed tonight. And, when he got home, he would still be David, but there was a difference now, and he only hoped it would be enough to get him through each day.

One last thing for Naomi and Boo, he thought, *and then I'll leave. I owe her. Maybe someday she'll even accept this payment.*

When he pulled up to The Clairemont, the sight of the dilapidated yet manicured hotel told him everything he needed to know about Bill Vassey. Most of the guy's money probably went toward child support, and an abrupt trip out to the West Coast was an expense that challenged his pocketbook.

David entered a small office decorated in cheap wood paneling with paintings of birds serving as atmosphere.

He went to the desk, where a young man was reading from an engineering textbook.

"I need to see Bill Vassey," David said. "And I know you can't give out the room number. Can you phone him?"

The student nodded, then carried out the request. He handed the phone to David after greeting Bill and telling him what was happening.

"I'm here to finish that talk," David said.

There was a pause on Bill's end. "Naomi's with you?"

"No. It's just me, and we need to hammer this out so that everyone benefits. I know you want to get back home, so the quicker, the better."

David took care to make sure he sounded rational, relatable, a negotiator rather than the enemy.

Yes, he was back, but it was for the sake of the woman and child who had captured his heart.

A heart that would never be the same again.

David steeled himself as Bill recovered from what was probably an unexpected proposition and answered.

"Okay, I'll meet you in the café."

They disconnected, and David asked the clerk for some paper and a pen, thanked him, then spotted the restaurant entrance down the hall.

He headed there, constructing every detail of what needed to be done.

Twilight spilled through the windows of the café, and David took a booth by the window, ordering coffee for both him and Bill, although he had no intention of touching it. The beverage was a signal of comfort, a psychological game that showed Bill that David was here to discuss, not accuse.

When the other man entered, David greeted him,

then went silent, waiting for Bill to sit before doing so, himself. He noticed that Naomi's ex had bloodshot eyes, perhaps from jet lag…but most likely from the stress of dealing with his own demons.

Bill spoke first, which is how David had always operated—setting the other party on edge so they felt compelled to erase the tension with noise.

"Understand something," the ex said, wrapping his hands around the coffee cup. "Naomi's a good girl. I just don't want what she does."

David wasn't here to persuade Bill to reconsider. No, he merely wanted the man gone forever.

And he knew just the way to do it, even if it meant lying again just to get Bill out of Naomi's life once and for all.

"You won't ever have to worry about her contacting you," he said and, for a naked moment, he even started believing what he was about to tell Bill. Just for one beautiful moment before he had to let go and face his own realities again, as Naomi said he should.

Her ex narrowed his eyes. "How can *you* guarantee that, Mr. Chandler? Are you speaking for Naomi?"

"Yes, I am." David lasered a gaze at the other man. "From this point forward, I'm assuming all responsibility for being her baby's father, and that child is never going to lack for anything. I'll sign the legal paperwork…everything. That makes you a free man, Bill."

And when David slid the blank piece of paper onto the table, writing down this promise—this method of getting Bill out of Naomi's life—he found that he truly did mean every word.

He would at least allow himself that before "David" fully claimed his rightful place once more.

Chapter Eleven

She couldn't believe what she was seeing.

Naomi leaned against an oak tree outside The Clairemont's café, watching David and Bill at a table, deep in intense conversation.

"You just rest easy," David had said before leaving her apartment. And…right. As if that were possible with the way things had been left dangling between them. So she'd walked the early-evening sidewalks, heading for the nearby motel where she hoped she would find her ex and the billionaire.

Billionaire.

She still couldn't absorb that because, to her, David Chandler would always be the guy who had chosen a family-style restaurant for one of their first "coffee outings." He would be the man who'd just about taken over her shift at Trinkets so she could "rest easy."

But, in reality, he was all about those crisp bills in his wallet.

A tycoon.

She tapped her fingers against the oak tree, focusing on Bill and Dave, or David or whoever he was. As she'd suspected a few minutes after he'd walked out her door, this meeting with her ex was what David had meant by not having to worry about Bill in the future.

But what exactly were they talking about?

She needed to go into the café and see for herself. But just as she was about to do that, the men got out of their windowside booth.

They shook hands, both of them stern.

At the strange sign of civility, Naomi's jaw almost hit the ground.

Afterward, Bill exited the restaurant, probably heading back to his room. He seemed relieved, his walk a little looser and liberated.

But David? He was stiffly dealing money onto the table for the bill, or maybe the tip. Then he picked up a piece of paper, read it over, and folded it neatly until it fit into his fine wallet.

When he made for the exit, she finally found her legs, moving into the parking lot in time to intercept him as he came out and headed for his rented SUV.

In a flash of discomfort, she wondered what he drove at home or if he was chauffeured all over the place instead—to the opera, five-star restaurants... billionaire places.

"Mind telling me what that was?" she asked as she approached him, trying not to sound accusatory.

Or judgmental.

She was so used to coping that way, but it had done more harm than good with both Dave and Bill. She'd finally learned that lesson the hardest way tonight.

At the sound of her voice, he stopped in his tracks, mere feet from his vehicle. He turned to her, and Naomi almost took a step back at the emotion in his eyes.

What was in his gaze? And why did she find herself unable to resist it, even though she should?

In the next instant, he seemed to lock himself up, the hue of his eyes icing to a pale blue. She had been responsible for bringing back this coldness that he'd wanted to shed. She knew that without a doubt.

God, what she would give to bring her Dave back.

"You want to know what I did?" David said simply. "I negotiated. It's what I'm best at."

His words sawed into her; it was as if he had given up on the purpose of his vacation altogether. His holiday as a new man—his attempt to find perspective, to improve himself—was over.

"I wish you wouldn't talk like that," she said.

"Like what?" Frigid, blank. "It was imperative that this Bill situation be taken care of."

"Then what did you do, David?" The urge to lay a hand on his arm, to just touch him again, was almost irresistible. But she kept to herself. He didn't seem to want any contact now, even though his eyes had begged for it earlier.

But when something cracked in his gaze, as if he wasn't sure what to say or how to react to her proximity, Naomi's pulse started jackhammering.

He seemed to notice, erecting that detached gaze again. "Bill won't be paying you any more visits. He won't be calling on the phone. He won't be a factor in your life from this night forward."

Stunned silence took the place of the air in her lungs.

Dave continued. "I'll be contacting my lawyers, and they'll draw up papers for Bill's agreement to cease and desist. Also, along with his official surrender of the child, you would have to agree to release him from all parental responsibility. The attorneys will untangle the legalities."

"All right," she said, head reeling.

How had Dave—no, David—managed this? Had the tycoon bought Bill off?

"Bill was pretty set in his ways," she said, testing, just as she would've if a curious object had dropped out of the sky to her feet. She would've poked at it, prodded. "It must've taken a lot to—"

"I didn't offer him money, if that's what you're thinking. If there's one thing I'm never going back to, it's using money to make myself feel important. That's not what I'm about anymore."

Mortification dripped from David's words, and she immediately wished he could take them back. She had clearly wounded *his* new sense of value now.

"I'm sorry I insinuated that," she said. "I really am."

A vein throbbed in his neck, and it seemed as if he were struggling to ignore the fact that she was standing just a foot away from him.

Did she actually matter that much to David?

"There were...other incentives that persuaded Bill," he continued. "Your ex wasn't after quick cash. This really was about extricating himself from further responsibility to you. That's the bottom line."

"But what could you have said that convinced him to back off?"

David seemed tortured, fighting with himself to withhold this particular information. "I…"

"David?"

He seemed to break, shaking his head. "I told myself I wouldn't skirt the truth anymore. Never again. Not with you."

Now she did rest her fingertips on his arm. At the contact, her heart jolted. "What did you do?"

He reached for her hand, then seemed to think better of it, stepping away so her hand dropped away from his arm.

Distant. Miles and miles from her.

"I told him," he said, "that I was assuming responsibility for Boo. That I was his or her dad, for all intents and purposes."

Naomi gasped, and it wasn't because he had taken such a step to get rid of Bill. No, it was because of the way David was watching her, his hopes naked in his gaze.

At her stunned hesitation, he cleared his throat, then pressed the alarm button on his key chain, obviously intending to leave now. The whoop of sound ripped the air in two, tearing an even bigger chasm between them.

"I was banking on the hope that this is what Bill wanted to hear," he said before she could get a word out, "and I was right. When the paperwork is ready, I'll be signing it, taking responsibility, just as promised. Then you can do with it what you will, Naomi, because I know how you'd probably feel about accepting aid."

She scrambled for words that wouldn't form.

Accepting help wasn't the issue. She was still trying to grasp what David had promised.

He was assuming the place of Boo's father?

He couldn't be serious. After all, he had a big life in New York to go back to. He wouldn't be ditching an American empire just because of what had transpired during one single vacation. People didn't do that kind of thing.

Did they?

She thought of what she had done—leaving Kane's Crossing in an effort to change, herself. But she hadn't been successful. Her old habits—judging people, lacking trust in them—had remained, and a switch of location hadn't been enough to encourage any life alterations.

But…could she change, too, just as David was trying to do?

Panic tumbled her stomach. The thought of abandoning her shelters scared her to death. Good Lord, she didn't have the courage.

His shoulders went even stiffer when she still couldn't find any words. He opened his car's door.

"Wait," she said. "David, I owe you so much that I don't think I can ever repay what you've done."

More. She'd wanted to say so much more, but she was terrified to.

He merely held on to the door, aiming a gaze so steeped in affection for her that she absently placed a hand over her chest.

"Just know," he said, "that falling for you and your child wasn't a part of any plan. And I never thought less

of you for all the stories you told about your past in
Kane's Crossing. Actually, I admire your love for a
child who could've suffered the same life you did, if
Boo didn't have a mother who cared so much. After I'm
gone, I hope you remember that."

He started to climb into the SUV, but Naomi, her
heart aching, her blood pumping, busted down her
barriers without even thinking.

"David, don't go."

She hadn't meant to say it, but there it was, out there,
an invitation to hurt.

An opportunity for yet another rejection.

He paused, as if catching up to what he'd just heard.

Naomi grabbed his T-shirt near the waist, knowing
that she had to make everything up to him.

Just as he had tried so hard to do in his own life.

Even through his shirt, David could feel the heat of
Naomi's touch. It recalled the imprint of her hand on his
stomach earlier today, when they had been so physically
intimate. It activated all those raw feelings he had come
to terms with as he'd held her, all the turmoil that he
needed to leave behind.

Because he would never improve Naomi's life. As
sure as the cool flow of Chandler blood creeping
through his veins, he was the guy he'd always been, and
there was no leaving him behind. Lying to her had been
the first clue. Negotiating with Bill about something as
precious as Naomi and Boo had only confirmed that.
Who the hell else on earth would've assumed responsibility for them as a bargaining chip?

Only David Chandler.

And that's who he was. Who he'd always be to some extent or another. Believing otherwise was a joke.

He maneuvered so that Naomi's fingers weren't making contact with his waist, but she still kept a hold on his shirt. Didn't she get it? He'd *lied* to her. She would remember soon enough.

Fortifying himself, he expelled a long-held breath.

"I've got to go, Naomi. We've both known that from the beginning."

At her destroyed expression, his gut fisted. Hurt, God, that had hurt. Without even knowing what he was doing, he touched her cheek, then pulled back, burned.

Why couldn't he stop himself?

"I wish this were easier," he said. "But there's business. Responsibility."

Each word was another pound of pressure on his shoulders, his chest. The weight had returned full force.

"You're important," she said. "I understand."

He expected her to turn around and cut off the discussion before it was resolved, just as she had done earlier when he'd tried to tell her his identity. Just as she'd done with Bill, as well.

But she stood her ground, rubbing a hand over an arm as if he'd bruised that, too, with his rejection.

Knowing he couldn't leave her like this, he shut and locked his car door, then reset the alarm. She'd walked here, he knew, and if it was the last thing he did, he would see her safely to her door. Besides, saying goodbye on a drive home didn't seem right.

"Come on," he said, gesturing toward the sidewalk with a jerk of his head, then walking toward it.

She followed, glancing back at the empty café, where

he had put all his chips on the table. Claiming Boo had seemed all-important at the time, since this was what Bill had wanted to be assured of. But…it had also seemed natural—so much a part of what was meant to be.

No matter. Now, in the arriving darkness of night, an odd bank of clouds slithered over the sky, and David Chandler knew better. When it came right down to it, he wasn't capable of providing love for anyone. He would always be a destroyer, no matter how much he longed for anything else.

"I suppose I shouldn't be shocked that this is happening," Naomi said, subtly wiping at her face. "You weren't ever going to stay."

"You wouldn't want me to anyway."

"How can you say that?"

She had halted by a large oak tree, its branches spreading over them like an ominous cover.

How could he spell this out? He didn't feel as if he deserved her, and he never would.

"Naomi, every time I looked at you, I'd think of how I failed you…how I failed *myself.*"

"You're not perfect, David. I'm not, either, and I'm sorry if I gave the impression that I expected that of you. God, I really have a way of doing that, don't I?"

"You have your reasons." He started walking again. It was hard to look at her even now. "*I* expected better of myself. I wanted to be more than a guy who can't come clean about his agendas."

"But you did come clean. At least, you tried before I sabotaged you."

There was no judgmental inflection, no chiding. That should've made him feel better, but it didn't.

"Lucas went through the same thing with his wife," David said, tracing his hand over a hedge, accepting the scratches as his due. "At my urging, my brother persuaded Alicia into a quick marriage, lying about the reason he wanted her to be with him. I take full responsibility for what happened, and one would've thought that I could learn from the entire ordeal. But in my passion for wanting to redeem myself, I went about it the wrong way."

The hedge ended, and David brushed his hands together, feeling the skin stinging. "I'll probably always go about it the wrong way, too. You don't need someone like that around."

"How do you know what I need?"

His blood pounded in remembrance of knowing what she'd needed this afternoon: caresses, kisses. But he didn't dare say it.

Naomi moved in front of him, walking almost backward so she could see his face. "I think you know exactly what I require, David. You knew when I asked you to come to the doctor's. You knew when you brought me breakfast and when you helped me in the store."

"My company owns Trinkets. Did *you* know that?"

There, that had gotten them back to the real problem.

As she took that in and allowed him to pass her, he increased his speed so he could get her home all the sooner. So he could end this anguished hunger to give in to his body, his impossible, no-doubt temporary emotions.

He kept himself on track, too, continuing the thread of his story. "We acquired the Trinkets chain in a hostile takeover of a corporation that owned everything from toy stores to candy companies to fast-food restaurants. I sat down to a posh meal at Jean Georges after the day closed out, and I never even thought about the people who were going to lose their jobs. They were collateral, all a part of doing business. Do you think that's the sign of a sensitive man?"

Her voice came from slightly behind him. "You never showed that side to me. I don't think you ever would've, either."

"I showed that side tonight when I met with Bill."

"No. Not unless you were lying about wanting to be a father to my child."

Words stuck in his chest.

By this time, they had come to the front of her apartment building, red brick faded in the climbing moonlight. He attempted to take strength from its cool solidness.

But when Naomi placed both hands on his arms and turned him toward her, he almost lost the battle at the sight of her beautiful, soulful eyes.

What exactly was he afraid of? Did he actually think that maybe the only thing he could *be* successful at was cutthroat business? Was he afraid to try anything else?

"You weren't lying when you told Bill you would be there for Boo," she said, voice strangled. "Were you, David?"

He couldn't say anything. Not if he wanted to get out of this in one piece.

"And you know what?" she asked. "That's the only truth that matters in the end. Do you realize that, even in the space of a little over a week, you've been more of a father to Boo than Bill ever was?"

Something chipped away inside of him, sending slivery debris against his chest.

Naomi gripped him tighter. "Being a dad isn't just

about conceiving a child. It's about being there. It's an investment of care, just like you've shown. And I should know. I never had a real dad, and one of the things I wished for all my life was someone who would build furniture for me or take me to pizza parlors or…just spend a little time with me." She drew even closer. "You've shown more affection to a child who still hasn't been born than I ever got after I was delivered."

That's because he adored the woman who carried Boo. It was true. Naomi showed him a different angle of life, a simpler pattern that eased his soul…if he even had one.

And that was a gamble he couldn't ask her to deal with.

At the thought, a chill swept over him. Even Naomi seemed to sense it, her hands dropping from his arms as she got that look in her eyes.

The anticipation of another betrayal.

See what he did to her?

"So *don't leave,*" she said again.

The wistfulness of her request almost had him. Almost.

"Naomi," he said, tone as even as he could manage, "have you ever asked yourself if maybe I'm just another Bill?"

A sound—a sob?—came from her, but she stood firm.

"Have you wondered," he continued, "if I could merely be another substitute for all the love you never got? You told me that's what Bill was to you, and you mistook it for more."

She was already shaking her head, as if in self-denial. Had he pushed the right button?

He hated himself right now, but that was nothing new. It was just something rediscovered.

She held up a finger, as if making the biggest point

she'd ever dared. "I'm not sure *what* I feel for you, David, but it's nothing like I've experienced before."

He stayed quiet, wanting to emphasize his point, too, but she must've mistaken his silence for a worse scenario. Her devastated expression told him that.

"You... You don't think I'm 'trading up,' like Bill said, do you?" she asked. "You don't think that I want to be with you because all those people who degraded me in the past would bite their tongues at the billionaire catch I've made. Please tell me you don't think that."

"Hell, Naomi, not at all."

He wanted to kick himself for going too far. He should've known that her ingrained doubts wouldn't disappear so quickly.

She laughed, a stinging sound. "Right. What would a man like you want with me anyway?"

He could list a million reasons—laughter he'd never enjoyed before, a new way of seeing the blue sky and, maybe most importantly, his own fleeting sense of value. She was gold and she had no idea.

Not knowing how to tell her this, he instinctively reached out for her instead.

Kissed her before he knew what he was doing.

She responded with a tiny wince, her palms against his chest not because she was pushing him away, but because he had surprised her and she'd gone off balance.

To remedy that, he swept his arms behind her, desperately holding her.

Gradually, her hands inched up until they were clasped around his neck.

Entwined.

Banded together.

They sipped at each other as the wind carried a trace of flowers from the window boxes on the street, of sunshine hiding in the darkness. Naomi pressed closer to him, seeking the warmth that only he could bring her, and she sighed against his lips.

Every question that had been racing around her head wisped away: why was he dwelling on such hard hurtful truths? Why did he seem like more of a stranger than even on that first day? Why...?

All she knew was that he felt so good, sending adrenaline in taut lines through her body. Fizzled yearning strung her together while yanking her apart, but all she wanted to do was extend the confused desire into months, years, decades.

She wanted Dave here, always and, at this moment, she would do anything to keep him.

But then, as he withdrew from her, those foster child pangs of alienation kicked away every positive thought, taking her over.

What made it even worse was Dave's supremely regretful expression as he stroked back her hair, his eyes running over her as if to memorize her face.

And when he placed a palm on her belly she knew what that kiss had really been about.

He backed away from her. "Goodbye," he said.

She looked into his eyes, caught in the soft, baby-blanket blue. She reached for his hand, but he was already too far away for her to connect.

Then, before her very gaze, he turned back into that ice man he'd told her about—the child of dysfunction who had learned how to cope just as she had.

"David?" she called as he began to walk away.

He didn't even bother to turn around as he stiffened, then said, "I'm not the guy you think I am."

Then he turned a corner and left her where they'd started on the day they'd met in The Suds Club.

Standing on her own, except for Boo.

Chapter Twelve

"I didn't even go after him," Naomi said to her friends at The Suds Club the next morning. "Even if that's all I wanted to do, I knew things wouldn't change, so I went back up to my apartment with my tail between my legs."

Mei and also Jenny, who had taken a personal day off work to prepare for a weekend business trip, listened diligently as their wash cycled. They were all huddled by the soda machine, keeping their voices low. It was a few hours until soap time, but the Laundromat was nevertheless crowded with excited social viewers who wanted to get their loads done before Dash and Trina faced off with übervillainess Delia. Everyone had even brought a potluck breakfast that Naomi had no appetite for.

"Are you going to call him?" Jenny asked, tucking a blond strand of hair behind her ear as she leaned forward.

"No." Mei, in opposition, leaned back, arms crossed.

"David thought it was amusing to play the identity game with Naomi. I don't see how that qualifies him for groveling."

"Hold on." Jenny again. "First off, Naomi wouldn't be groveling. Going after what you want does not equal a show of begging. Second, I don't think he was 'playing,' as you put it. From what Naomi says, he never intended any harm, and that makes all the difference, if you ask me."

"Naomi agrees with that," Naomi said. "Remember, I'm right here in the room, too?"

Both of the other women focused on their friend, smiling apologetically.

Mei swept her hand out to Naomi, in a take-the-floor gesture.

But what else did she have to say? She felt like a wind-up toy that had come up against a wall, her motor running down as she kept walking into an immovable barrier.

She popped her quarters into the beverage machine, pushing the button for a bottle of water. "Waiting around isn't sitting right with me. I keep thinking that David's at his hotel, packing up his things so he can go on the road or home or…wherever."

"Call him then," Jenny said.

Leaning against the machine, Naomi twisted off the top of her bottle, deliberating, even though she knew darned well what she wanted to do. Her body was keening for it, even as her brain told her to let him go.

Jenny continued. "You did go through a lot together, even in a short time. It would stink to leave things as they are now." She got out her cell. "What's his number?"

"Wait." Naomi stood straight. "I just…I can't…"

Both women furrowed their brows at Naomi.

"You can't what?" Mei asked.

Another Suds Club member strolled into their midst, and Naomi moved away from the machine so Vivian— the married woman with the seven-year-old birthday girl—could buy a drink.

"I couldn't help overhearing," the biker-short-wearing mom said while depositing her coins. "Are you talking about Dave over here?"

"David," Mei said.

Vivian fanned herself. "Go get him, Naomi. What in blazes are you waiting for with a hunk like that?"

Naomi blinked. Truthfully, she was waiting for that destructive judgmental habit of hers to dissipate so she could trust someone else. She was waiting for lightning to strike.

But then she thought of how she had actually been willing to work through his identity lie last night. How he had kissed her so tenderly. How she had felt such a loss after he had left.

She had already been struck, hadn't she?

Good Lord, she… Yes, she *loved* him. But she hadn't been able to open her heart all the way, instead setting him up for failure with her high expectations and inability to give someone like him an opportunity to make things right.

She hadn't been able to admit that her heart was his until he was gone.

"He's the best man I've ever met," Naomi said. "Even if he won't see that himself."

He just needed to be set free from his own self-perceptions, she thought. Just what he'd helped her to accomplish.

"Get thee to his hotel then," Vivian said, reaching down to where her soda had clunked into the chute.

"But…" Naomi plucked at her skirt. Nerves. "What if he reacts the same way he did last night?"

Jenny stood. "Then I guess you've got to convince him to stay."

"Win him over," Vivian added. "And, above all, make him think it was *his* idea. That's key."

She was right, Naomi realized. David had already accepted her—that had been obvious from his heartfelt confessions. The problem was in how he saw himself.

So how was she going to manage to win him over?

Naomi's blood fizzed with anxiety. Anticipation.

"Don't fret," Mei said, standing, as well, then putting her arm around her friend's shoulders. "We'll give you a pep talk if you're really going to do this."

Mei's own marital problems seemed to surface in her concerned gaze. *Are you sure you want to do this?* she seemed to ask.

Yes, Naomi realized. More than anything.

"Ooh," the happily married Vivian said, seeming way too excited about this single-girl intrigue. Things must've been slow around the house with her kids in school and her husband at work. Or maybe she was just a sucker for romance. "Let's have a brainstorming session."

Naomi released a shaky breath, then nodded resolutely. The notion of David deserting her and Boo made her think of that toy endlessly banging against the wall, losing all energy and dying.

But when she thought of seeing him again…

It felt as if she were being wound up anew, whirring with happiness and excitement about what might happen if she could persuade him that he really was the right man for her and Boo.

"Nothing ventured," she said, "nothing gained."

Vivian held up her hand for a high five. "That's the spirit."

Hence, Jenny and Mei huddled with Naomi and Vivian, formulating a plan. A final attempt to win David back.

In his hotel room, David hung up his cell, disconnecting from the conversation he'd been having with his lawyers.

All morning he had ironed out the Bill-Naomi situation, also faxing his own signed promise to the legal team. He had additionally made arrangements to fly them to Kane's Crossing, where they would accommodate Bill once he arrived there tonight.

Now, all David had to do was wait for word from them and for the rest of his life to continue. He refused to summon any of the Chandler jets—it just didn't seem palatable after what had gone down in Placid Valley—so he used his old open-ended ticket to book a seat on the commercial airline's first flight to New York. The earliest available departure was tonight, and David needed to pack if he was serious about hopping on it.

Rising from his spot on the bed, he decided to deal with the maid's tip first. He reached for the envelope on the nightstand then opened his wallet, extracting some well-worn bills. As he ran a thumb over the money, he realized that it wasn't so crisp anymore.

Shoving the cash into the envelope, he tossed it on the bed, then turned to his barely used road map. Maybe, instead of flying back to New York, he could randomly pick a spot to travel to next.

Or was that just an excuse to put off the inevitable?

All he really wanted to do was stay right here, where his ears were perked for a knock on his door or a call on his phone. But, hell, Naomi wouldn't contact him again. In fact, if he were her, he would stay as far away as possible.

Every step, every motion seemed to drag as he packed, then kicked back to watch TV, killing more time. Maybe he would go to the airport early and mingle with all the other people in transit. People who were in limbo, as well.

Then he came across *Flamingo Beach,* and he lost the will to move.

All he could see was Naomi's lively gaze as she filled him in on the star-crossed lovers, Dash and Trina, at the coffee place, then at the Laundromat. The memories captured David, and he clung to them, knowing they were all he had left of her.

But when a knock sounded at his door, he was forced to give those up, too.

"Room service," said a male voice.

Since David hadn't ordered anything, he got up to glance through the peephole.

Indeed, there stood a suited man with a mustache, hovering over a linen-draped cart with one covered food tray.

David propped the door open. "I think you have the wrong room."

The waiter peered at his order tablet. "David Chandler, yes?"

"Yeah, but I'm checking out soon. Late check-out."

"Oh, but, sir, it's food. Good food." The man offered a toothy smile.

Then, without warning, the waiter pushed the cart forward, and David reacted by stepping out of the way.

"Good eats," the man said. "And it's compliments of a friend. She made arrangements with the kitchen."

David's pulse jerked. "A...friend?"

"Yes, sir." Lifting the lid off the solitary dish, the waiter exposed a platter of what looked to be corn bread. "She requested something simple to start off with, yet there is more to come if you wish."

When David offered a completely puzzled look, the man pointed at a card next to the bread plate.

"For you," he said. "Have a good day, sir."

He refused a tip on the way out, saying it was covered, then left David alone with the...corn bread.

As he reached for the envelope, he got light-headed.

What was Naomi doing?

When he opened the card, warmth slid through him. The beginning of an artic melt that he couldn't allow.

Let's not end on a sour note. How about a friendly goodbye?

The handwriting was painstakingly neat, the signature as curvy as a riotous bunch of soft hair.

Naomi.

Why was she drawing this all out? She should be leaving well enough alone, not making it harder for him to get away.

His first instinct was to call her up, thank her for her troubles, but deny her. Yet, damn it, that was the last thing he really wanted to do.

Realistically, he owed her a friendly meeting, didn't he?

He noticed a P.S. at the bottom of the card.

Enjoy the appetizer. It's not exactly the Kentucky corn bread I like to make, but you get the idea.

His stomach was in too much chaos to handle food, and when another knock shook his door, the sensation was multiplied.

This was it, he thought. This was where he would have to face Naomi and suffer the politeness of a much more positive farewell.

Armoring himself, he used the peephole again, but when he saw another man—a bellhop—standing there instead, disappointment consumed him.

Nonetheless, he opened up.

"For you, sir," the young man said, handing David a manila envelope, which was heavier than it first appeared.

This guy, too, refused a tip, leaving David to shut the door and open the message.

What he found almost floored him.

It was a copy of Boo's ultrasound picture, enlarged and placed in a frame you could buy at any store.

Except, to David, it was priceless.

A little note was taped to the wood.

Meet us at 1:30 p.m. by the lobby doors for the rest of the meal.

As if he would refuse *now*. Damn, she knew how to persuade.

He would just take care to keep himself in check. That's all. He had already decided what was best for her, and there was no changing his mind.

Still, he informed the desk of when he would be leaving, dawdled some more by watching a local talk show featuring some movie fanatics wielding light sabers, then made sure his hair was combed before going downstairs. There, he officially checked out and left his luggage with the bellhops, coming to the lobby doors at the appointed time. Hell, maybe he was even a little early, but he did find a cab idling by the curb.

Good God, Naomi didn't have the money to be doing this stuff.

"David Chandler?" the female cabbie asked as he got in.

He confirmed, even though the name was starting to sound more like another memory than anything else.

She drove him a short way to a park in Naomi's neighborhood: it boasted freshly cut green grass, a white gazebo, flower beds and iron-and-wood benches along the meandering stone trails. After dropping him off, she informed him that she was booked to pick him up so he could retrieve his luggage at the hotel then go to the airport.

As she departed, he turned to the park, his blood flow coming to a screeching halt.

Because there, over the slight swell of a grassy hill, stood Naomi.

Her flowery skirt belled in the breeze as she clasped her hands behind her back. She was watching him carefully, as if expecting him to walk away again.

But how could he? There was no place he would rather be.

Hey, remember—you've already made up your mind, his ice man chimed. *You can be gracious, but don't let her in.*

David made sure his defenses were intact, then approached her.

Coming closer, he noticed that her gaze had a yearning sheen about it, and that was almost enough to break him.

No.

"Hi," she said rather shyly.

"Hi, yourself." He itched to touch her curls, to enclose her in his arms.

No!

"I'm glad you came." She motioned for him to follow her.

Once they were over the hill, he discovered a picnic blanket, a basket, plates and plastic glasses.

"You don't play fair, Naomi," he said. "That picture of Boo? Pure emotional hijacking. "

"I figured a memento wouldn't come amiss," she said with a grin. "Besides, I really want to set us to rights again. This way, we get to end with a good memory."

He must've seemed doubtful, so she laid it out for him.

"No heavy discussion allowed during our picnic," she said. "No 'what-if's or 'if only's. Just two friends celebrating the nice times they had together. Deal?"

He had faced off with the best negotiators in the world, but they were amateurs compared to Naomi.

"Deal," he said.

She motioned toward the blanket, and they both took a seat on the ground.

"In keeping with the whole country corn bread theme," she said, "I've got some cheese grits, fried apple pies and salt-cured ham with biscuits. Just like a Sunday meal in Kane's Crossing."

The hominess appealed to David, tugging at him. "You shouldn't have."

"Oh, but I did." She loaded a plate with the vittles, handing it over to him when she was done. "I was short on time this afternoon, but there's a great take-out Southern place across town that Mei drove me to. Rest assured, though—I really can cook like this in my own kitchen."

She sounded so proud.

As he ate, he found himself smiling, without that weight on his shoulders or chest now. The food was damn good stuff that could put a lot of happy-pounds on a man.

"How did you know that I hadn't left town yet?" he asked between mouthfuls and grateful comments.

"Turns out that one of the girls at The Suds Club knows someone who knows someone else who works at your hotel. He looked your status up as a friend favor. It's all very 'small town' of them."

"Sure is," he muttered.

"I'm sorry, David, I know it was presumptuous."

In security terms, it was alarming, but he didn't care this time. Not when Naomi had only the best intentions.

She kept talking, as if to make sure the conversation didn't stray anywhere uncomfortable.

"Small towns," she said, ripping off a piece of

biscuit. "Even with everything that happened in Kane's Crossing, I do miss certain things about it. When you hear people talking about rolling green hills, they're not exaggerating. You ever seen Kentucky?"

"Never had the pleasure."

"I bet you'd like those hills. They give you a sense of…" She tilted her head. "All I can think to say is… 'aah.' Because that's how it feels to be looking at them."

He set his fork down, enraptured by the flow of her words, her sweet voice.

"The town has all these odd local legends, too, like a story about a mermaid who lives in Cutter's Lake. There are old-timers who swear she's real, and that they've seen her by moonlight. The town even has a glass castle, if you can believe that. And there are haunted houses aplenty."

Her eyes were sparkling again, and Dave was fully drawn out of David's shell. But when he realized it, he tried to recover.

It took a hell of a lot of effort, but he did it.

Yes, he thought sadly, as the weight returned to settle over him. He sure did it.

And she seemed to notice, her gaze dimming ever so slightly. Still, she continued her light discussion, almost as if both of them fully believed that this really was a casual picnic.

In the meantime, Dave pounded at David's chest, screaming to get out.

Naomi's plans were falling apart.

She was trying so hard to be persuasive, yet subtle enough to bring David around. He *had* to come to a realization that he was a better man than he gave himself credit for—that was the point of all this. And, through experience, she knew that if she told him he was warm and giving, it wouldn't matter.

He needed to believe it, and she had hoped that seeing her one last time—without any pressure—would do the trick.

But it hadn't.

Still, she soldiered on, unwilling to give up on him.

"I'd love to raise Boo in a small town setting," she said, nibbling at her biscuit. "There really are a lot of positives about that. A sense of security, quiet nights where the stars can shine their brightest without the city lights muting them."

David bent his knees, leaning his forearms on his thighs while looking into the near distance. "The city has its high points, too. Culture, with all the art galleries, the best that the theater has to offer."

Was he trying to convince himself?

"Smog-choked air," she countered.

"Opportunities, chances for a new start," he parried right back.

They faced off. But when he smiled, as if he'd just been messing with her, she didn't buy it.

She had to get him back. And it was time to play that trump card she'd already pulled out.

"Can you imagine what Boo could be in either place?" she asked.

He glanced at his knees, as if refusing to look into her eyes and be captured.

But then, as if in spite of his grand efforts, a gentle smile tipped his lips, and it raised Naomi's spirits, too.

"I imagine he or she will be the smartest kid in class," he said. "A leader that everyone will look up to. He or she will have the lion heart of her mama, as well."

His smile was weighted with what she thought might be melancholy.

"I wish I knew if Boo was a he or she," he said quietly.

God, she wished he would be around to know that, too, holding her hand as the sex was announced.

It would be a celebration, just as he had said back in the doctor's office. Another reason to rejoice.

"I could always let you know," Naomi said. "What I mean is, I could send a postcard with the news, if you wanted me to."

He closed his eyes, as if warding off the possibility. A muscle clenched in his cheek.

"I don't know if that's a good idea," he said.

She tried not to slump at his refusal. But what else could she do to guide him toward opening his arms to her? Was this just a losing battle?

"Okay," she finally said, "but you can always change your mind."

He picked up his plate again, and they ate in strained silence. A little boy ran by, pulling a kite behind him. It was painted to resemble a sparrow, Naomi saw, and it was finding its wings and spreading them.

Seconds later, an elderly man and woman walked by on the path, their steps unsure as they linked arms. They nodded at Naomi and David, clearly thinking they were having a lovely picnic. She did her best to smile back at them.

Yet when she did, the tears crept up on her. Shoot,

these hormones were killing her, but then again, she could always put the blame on them for what felt like a slowly breaking heart.

All too soon, David had finished his plate, declining more. The little boy ran by with his kite again, laughing until it suddenly caught a troubled burst of wind and took a nosedive to the ground.

Out of the corner of Naomi's eye, she saw the taxicab pull in to the second parking lot, where she had instructed the driver to go this time.

David saw it, too.

"Well…" he said, standing.

Naomi also rose to her feet, unsteady. Legs shaking.

"Well…" she repeated.

He hesitated and, for a sublime moment, she thought she saw his true, bared self peering out at her from those blue, blue eyes. She felt alive—so alive at seeing the man she loved.

But when David straightened his posture and stuck out his palm for a handshake, Naomi went dark inside.

"I'll make sure everything goes smoothly with Bill," he said.

It couldn't end like this. But she wouldn't ask him to stay again. That would do no good unless he believed in himself enough to make the choice to be with her on his own.

"Thank you, Dave," she said, emphasizing the nickname, as if to conjure him back. "We're going to miss you."

He started to turn around, but then pivoted back to enfold her in an all-encompassing embrace.

She reveled in it, taking in his scent, his warmth, until he pulled away.

Then he headed to the taxi without saying another word.

Chapter Thirteen

Without much energy, Naomi packed up the picnic and went home, unable to believe the outcome of her crusade to win David over.

It wasn't that he had denied her because she wasn't good enough. No, she was beyond thinking that way now; throughout their better days, David had shown her that she could be so much more than a cast-off child.

It was that he had walked away as troubled as he had come.

Heart heavy, she got ready for work, donning clothes that seemed tighter than they'd ever been before.

But it wasn't the clothes that made her weep.

Finally giving in to all her disappointment, she allowed herself the freedom of cleansing herself with the tears. She even tried to soothe Boo by reclining on the couch and rubbing her belly.

"Don't worry, sweetheart," she whispered. "We're as strong as David told us we were, even without him."

Yet as she resolved to go to her late shift and march on with life, her reassurances sounded so empty.

Nevertheless, after taking one last moment to compose herself, Naomi rose to her feet, walked across the room, then opened the door.

But what she saw in front of her forced her to grip the frame. It was all she could do to survive the blast of surprised exultation.

He was standing there. David. Only a few feet away, his hands on his hips, his expression tortured.

"I...couldn't leave," he said, voice ragged. "I got to the airport and I knew that boarding that plane was the last thing I could bring myself to do. But when I got here, I couldn't knock, either. At first, I paced outside your apartment, calling the owner of Trinkets and telling him that you'd need a replacement on your shift tonight."

From a faraway spot in her muddled brain, she realized that David Chandler's company owned Trinkets and he could get her off work if he wanted to.

And...he had wanted to?

He went on, words like a train headed for a crash. "Then I made it up the elevator, and I've been outside your door for the last twenty minutes, asking myself if I'm doing the right thing."

She couldn't grasp this. David was *here?*

He hadn't gotten on that plane?

When he hesitated, watching her with that tormented expression, everything cleared up for Naomi.

"This is the rightest thing anybody has ever done,"

she said, holding open the door, heart palpitating at the offer she was making.

A permanent invitation.

She backed into her apartment, pulling him with her.

It was at this moment that she knew he had definitely come back to her—and it had been *his* idea—but the man she loved was still buried. Yes, he was trying to claw his way out, but it was up to Naomi to help him the rest of the way.

She shut the door and he walked across the room to a wide, plush couch that she often fell asleep on while watching TV. With every step, she saw his doubts grow, his limbs go stiffer as he planted those hands on his hips again.

His admiral pose, she thought. She recalled it from their first meeting.

But that had been "David," she knew, and "Dave" was reaching out to her.

"When I thought you'd caught that plane back to New York," she said, "I felt like someone had reached into my chest and yanked out a part of me."

Those hands on his hips seemed to brace themselves even harder against what she was saying, but she could tell that whatever was holding him back was losing the battle.

"I don't know much," she said, coming closer, "but I'm sure of one thing, and that's how I've come to feel about you. I love you, Dave."

She heard him draw in a breath.

Don't stop now.

"And loving you has nothing to do with making up for what I never got in the past," she added, her heart-beat pumping in her ears so loudly that her words

sounded as if they'd been packed in cotton, just like trea-
sured valuables. "It has everything to do with how you
make me smile, how you care for me as if I'm some
precious, one-of-a-kind person. It has to do with how I
know you'll love Boo unconditionally, unwaveringly.
Unselfishly."

"And what if I decide that I'm going to be someone
else tomorrow? What if I can't hold on and I return to
wonderful David Chandler form?"

"Why would you ever go back to being the man who
worked people over for his own benefit? Do you enjoy
being that person?"

"No." He slowly shook his head. "I don't."

"Then why are you still acting like him?"

He jerked, then turned all the way around to her. The
power of his presence seared her.

"What if," he said, voice so low and level that it
shook her, "this new man fails? What happens after
that? Who would you be left with?"

"I would only be worried about that if I thought you
were putting on an act. Now, I know that my instincts
haven't been absolutely on target in the past, but this
time, I'm right. And no matter how much you want to act
like there isn't some warm spot inside you, blazing its
way out, I know you feel something for me. Maybe it's
not love yet, but it can grow. I have faith in that. In you."

"Oh, Naomi." His gaze softened. "Do you have
faith in what the press would do if they got wind of
our relationship?"

This was his last stand, she thought. He had brought
out *his* trump cards.

Her hands started to tremble as she recalled Bill recognizing David Chandler. A tycoon, a New York power-house. He lived in a different world that he wouldn't entirely be able to escape, even with a thousand vacations.

"First off," he said gently, "they're going to dig into your past because they'll be curious about the woman David Chandler has brought home. My brother's redeemed-playboy story has worn thin with them, but their eyes are still on the family. Would you be ready for *that?*" he asked.

She searched his face, trying to find any hint of shame that he might express at how she'd grown up, at the bad choices she had made.

But she also saw a well of inspiration in the dark centers of his eyes. David—no. To her he was, and would always be, Dave. Dave didn't think she was that girl. He truly didn't. And he probably never had.

"Why would I be ashamed?" she asked. "Why would what they say matter if I've gotten past all that?"

"They're tough. They don't let up."

"Not even if they were to see how much I adore you?"

He bent his head. "You have no idea what you're asking for."

"Yes, I do. You just don't want to give in because you're scared to death that you'll disappoint me. But unless you're hiding more surprises, I'm not sure how that could ever happen. Boo and I love you—*need* you—too much to *let* it happen."

She held out her hand to him.

But accepting her hand wouldn't be a casual gesture. It would mean accepting everything that went along with it.

Even so, Naomi didn't move a muscle, making her own last stand.

* * *

At the admission that she needed him, David—or was it truly Dave now?—felt his self-control sliding away. Naomi could persuade him like no other human on earth, and that should've been impossible.

It should've been horrifying.

But…it wasn't. He was flailing to keep himself intact out of mere habit, yet now that he had no arguments left, he realized that resisting was useless.

Not when he wanted more than anything to tell this woman that he loved her, too.

The confession banged to get out; it was the last vestige of the man he'd always known and, even though "David" needed to be buried, the notion of letting him go was frightening because "Dave" had no track record. "Dave" wasn't predictable.

Or maybe he was. Maybe he was the most dependable man a woman like Naomi could ever want.

The hopeful glimmer in her gaze told him that he was right, that she thought he really was deserving of her and Boo.

As the heat of her love crept into him, filling him, Dave shed the last of his doubts, pulling Naomi by the hand toward him so he could embrace her.

"I love you, too," he whispered, committing to this new life.

This new love.

At his hard-won confession, Naomi buried her face against Dave, breathing him in, out, and in again. It was as if she were holding him within her body, feeling him become a part of her.

But he wanted more than this. He wanted to show

her—show *himself*—that he trusted them both. That they had made the right choices this time.

No more doubts…ever.

He smoothed a hand over her back. Curves, grace, all woman.

All his.

"So I don't have to go to work tonight?" she said against his chest.

His pulse picked up, just like footsteps walking, then running toward a final destination.

"You don't have to be anywhere." He trailed his hands down her back. "Just with me, Naomi. Truly just with me."

"Good, because I was going to have to work an extra day this weekend to make up for these part-time nights I've been stuck with." In spite of the lightness, it came out a cracked whisper.

She slipped her hands under his T-shirt, touching the skin of his back, and he moaned a little.

Clearly encouraged, she slid her fingers to the front of him, exploring his abs. He hitched in a breath.

"You feel good," she said.

When she traced up to his chest, coming to stop at his nipples, he softly grunted.

"This is your favorite spot?" she asked.

"Just one of them."

Swept away, he kissed her—long and lovingly, as if they had all the time in the world.

And…damn. They truly did.

The thought released him, and he used his tongue to deepen the exchange. He tasted her, reveled in her, wanted her more than ever now that he knew he was here to stay.

They came up for air, their fingers entangled in hair and clothing.

"If I had met you a couple months earlier," she said between breaths, "Boo could've been your child."

"As far as I'm concerned, he or she *is* mine."

Joy filtered through Naomi's gaze, and she swept a hand down Dave's chest, to his belly. There, she traced the line of down that led to a part of him that was already growing hard, excited.

He didn't stop her. All he wanted was to pretend as if tonight would be Boo's conception, that the love between him and Naomi had created such a wonderful combination of them both—a legacy who would grow to make them proud.

As she stroked down farther, mapping his growing tumescence, a gush of heat flooded his groin, stiffening him even more. He strained against his jeans, so swollen he didn't know how long he could wait.

"I'll be gentle," he said, "don't worry."

She cupped him, and one of his hands tightened on her arm.

They kissed again and, unlike last time, when he had been too much of a gentleman to push their encounter, he took charge, lifting her up and plastering her against him. He moved back toward the oversize couch, then laid her down.

He crouched over Naomi; her gaze burned with a desire that he could read like the temperature. Then, he rested a hand on her collarbone, easing it downward over her shirt in slow, hungry exploration until he came to a breast.

Sucking in her breath at the painful and stimulating

contact, she raised a hand over her head while he circled her nipple with a thumb.

Then, just as she stirred with restless longing for more, he stroked downward, over her stomach, her belly, between her legs.

She bucked, groaned, as he pressed his knuckles against her, then adjusted his position so he could slip both his hands under her skirt. Her thighs felt like satin sheets on a warm night.

"You have the smoothest skin," he said.

As he guided his hands to her inner thighs, their breathing filled the room with strained rhythm.

"Oh, Dave," she said, riding another groan.

A climax was obviously building inside of her, and she grabbed a pillow near her head.

As he pulled off her panties, his thumb brushed between her legs. She was damp, ready.

Unable to contain himself, he parted her legs, then coaxed a finger, then two, into her as she let out a tiny cry.

Swirling and thrusting, he manipulated her with his thumb, as well. Her hips writhed along with the cadence, and a pressure began to build within him, too. It climbed up and up until a sob broke out of her lungs and pushed him higher than he'd ever gone before without bursting.

That sob seemed to bubble, then expand in the air, making it thick with primal heat, making him increase the speed of his ministrations.

Dave watched the pleasure on her face glow as she closed her eyes, hips arching higher and higher until she convulsed, her passage tightening around his finger.

While she came down, he withdrew, his body so

tense and ready that he thought he might explode. He had been waiting his whole life for a time when his emotions would weave through the physical aspect of being with a woman, and that moment was here.

It scared him.

Thrilled him.

Wanting to draw out this profound show of their love, he unbuttoned her blouse as she focused in on him, her eyes hazy.

"What about you?" she asked on a lazy, breathless sigh.

"I'm fine." He separated the material until her modest white bra peeked out.

She pushed herself up, perspiration gleaming on her dusky skin. "Yeah, Dave, you're fine, all right. And it's my turn to appreciate just how fine you are."

He delighted in the change in atmosphere. No more doubts and darkness—everything was light, with the world stretching out before them.

In a jarring moment of realization, he found that he liked the idea of living that way: without a harried sense of duty, without nights in a lonely bed.

In fact, he loved it.

Naomi grabbed the hem of his T-shirt. "Let me take care of things now."

Before he knew quite what was happening, she pulled the material upward, encouraging him to lift his arms so she could take off his shirt. Hair ruffled, he laughed as she placed a hand on his bare chest and forced him to his back.

"Relax," she said, working off his boots now.

He relaxed, all right, propping a pillow beneath his head while she got him out of everything except for his boxers.

Then Naomi sat on his outstretched legs; she had tucked her skirt under her, all ladylike.

Using her hand to mold his chest, she sighed again, clearly pleased.

"You're a vision, Dave. Just an absolute vision."

She rubbed one of his nipples, and he flinched. Sensitive. They had always been his weak spot.

But she knew that.

With playful precision, she bent to him, licking him there. Then, as he fought to control himself, she kissed her way downward, stopping at his belly, where his muscles jumped at the touch of her soft lips. She raised herself up, making eye contact as she guided him out of the boxers.

Ready, so ready for her.

Warming him against her hands, she said, "I want you so badly, Dave."

Her eyes drove the point home. *I love you,* they said, *and I trust you with my very soul.*

"I love you, too," he said, his voice sounding as if it had been dragged over the ground until it bled the truth.

A smile so intensely beautiful that he thought he might die from the happiness of it lit over her face. She stood, then took off her blouse, her bra, her skirt.

And there she was, naked in body and spirit, offering him everything he couldn't refuse. Not anymore.

He got to his feet, too, removing his boxers and taking only a moment to retrieve a condom from his wallet before going to her.

She touched his hand. "Do we need that now?"

Was she thinking about how condoms tended to break anyway? Of how she no doubt wanted to feel him bare inside her just as much as he did?

"No, we don't," he said, tossing the packet away. "I've got a clean bill of health."

"Me, too."

Then, unable to wait a second longer, he swept Naomi up into his arms so he could carry her to the bed.

A marriage bed, he thought, because this was their first union. A vow that they would be together forever.

After he eased her down, she kicked back the spread and sheets, baring the mattress, too. He covered her with his body, his skin alive, his heart beating so hard that it took over his mind.

Flesh to flesh, he managed to think, before a cloud of need and ecstasy consumed him.

When he entered her, she grabbed onto him, as if her very life depended on him being inside. He felt the same way as he moved in, out, the rhythm easy as her hips ground into him.

Careful, so careful, not to hurt Boo or even Naomi. Still, his body demanded a faster, harder tattoo, so he raised himself up on his arms to keep from crushing her.

An image had misted over his sight: iced rocks being lifted off him, one by one. Off his chest, his shoulders, like a punished man being set free.

Yet, at the same time, his body pounded, getting tighter, needing a release....

Naomi urged him on, straining, soaring and making tiny noises that told him she was about to explode, too.

And when she did, it ripped at him.

With an inner roar, he seemed to fly open, busting out of every constraint, his skin raw and burned to expose what had been underneath, battling all this time to get out.

But then, as he turned to liquid, he fell to Naomi's side and held her to him.

A new man exposed, he thought, pressing his lips against the forehead of the woman he loved.

A born husband and father.

Epilogue

Ten months later...

The most recent winter and spring seasons in New York had seen their share of storms, but Dave, Naomi and Boo—or Barbara, as they had named their child—had outlasted them all.

As the sun ushered in an early summer's day, they pulled up to Ford Chandler's East Hampton "getaway cottage," which was actually an Old World 1920s gray three-story mansion worth ten million dollars. One block from the beach, it was surrounded by sheltering trees while a massive Roman pool glittered beneath the sky.

Dave got out of the SUV he had bought upon returning to New York with Naomi, then went around to guide her out of the passenger seat. Laughing, she fell against him, kissing him as he hugged her.

"Hey," he said, smiling down at her when they were done, "what do you think this is, a honeymoon?"

"It isn't too soon for another one, you know," she said.

Upon leaving Placid Valley, he had purchased a condo in Manhattan—but nothing as fancy as his relinquished bachelor pad. He and Naomi had moved in soon afterward, already having been married at a small civil ceremony right around the time he had taken care of the paperwork to formally adopt Boo.

"I hear you," Dave said, giving her one last kiss. "And I'm up for as many honeymoons as you want."

Still smiling at her while he went to the back door, Dave couldn't stop the glow that infused him. Naomi, Mrs. Chandler. His good fortune amazed him every day, every hour.

The aroma of barbecue traveled the air, and his wife sniffed, holding her clasped hands to her chest in utter joy.

"They've got steaks on again," she said.

"Lucas is probably playing Lord Grillmaster." But Dave didn't say it with any resentment. He'd learned so much from Naomi and Boo, including how to accept being on equal footing with his half brother.

Because as far as Dave was concerned, he was the luckiest man in the universe, and no one could touch that.

In fact, Dave had decided to relinquish most of his duties at The Chandler Organization while staying on as a consultant. He wanted to be with his new family, most of all. Two years ago, the withdrawal would've eaten away at him, but not now.

One of the reasons for this turnabout peered up at him through sleepy eyes after Dave opened the back door.

Boo.

She looked just like Naomi, with her olive gaze and bright smile—one that was aimed right at him as he stood there, struck dumb with adoration. He'd been there for her birth, been there every second because he was truly her father.

As he unstrapped her from the backward-facing car seat, he took care to support her neck. So fragile. He always worried that she might fall apart, even though he knew she was as tough as her mom.

He settled her into the crook of his arm while Naomi grabbed the diaper and odds-and-ends bags. Then, when she finished, she stopped to stare at her husband and daughter, her eyes welling up.

"You're a real picture, you two," she said.

He held out his other arm to her, and she came to them, tickling Boo under the chin—the baby loved that—and nestling against Dave as he walked them to the "cottage's" front door.

They rang the bell and, within a minute, they were greeted by both Gabriel and Phoebe.

Damp bathing suits gave testament to their pool activity as they hugged their aunt and uncle, then jumped up and down while trying to get a good look at their cousin.

"Whoa!" said a female voice.

With an armload of towels, Alicia came scooting in to the foyer, her long dark hair in a ponytail. She tossed a couple towels to the kids, indicating that they needed to wrap themselves up.

At the same time, she gave a "Welcome!" to Dave and his family, embracing them.

But Dave's mind wasn't entirely on her greeting—

not when Lucas and his father were standing near the foyer entrance.

As in David's old fantasies, he saw Ford Chandler smiling in approval, his faded blue eyes glistening as he leaned on his cane.

And, although Dave didn't need Ford's validation any longer, it was fulfilling. He smiled back at his father, content and complete.

Even Lucas, who towered over their dad, was full of happiness for his brother. He came forward to give Dave a man-hug as Alicia and Naomi segued into talking about the charity event they were embarking upon this week.

Value, Dave thought. The volunteer work that Alicia was getting Naomi involved in brought out even more sparkle in his wife, and seeing her spread her wings brought him to just another level of heaven.

And when Naomi turned to him amidst all the cheery chaos, his heart lit up like the center of a sun that had come to shine over both of them.

A man and a woman who had ventured out of the darkness to finally find themselves, as well as each other—that's what they were.

A husband, a wife, an entire family he'd found…and embraced.

* * * * *

Look for Mei's story,
THE SECOND-CHANCE GROOM,
the second book in
Crystal Green's new miniseries
THE SUDS CLUB.
Coming in June to Silhouette Special Edition

Enjoy a sneak preview of
MATCHMAKING WITH A MISSION
by B.J. Daniels,
part of the
WHITEHORSE, MONTANA *miniseries.*
Available from Harlequin Intrigue
in April 2008.

Nate Dempsey has returned to Whitehorse to uncover the truth about his past....

Nate sensed someone watching the house and looked out in surprise to see a woman astride a paint horse just on the other side of the fence. He quickly stepped back from the filthy second-floor window, although he doubted she could have seen him. Only a little of the June sun pierced the dirty glass to glow on the dust-coated floor at his feet as he waited a few heartbeats before he looked out again.

The place was so isolated he hadn't expected to see another soul. Like the front yard, the dirt road was waist-high with weeds. When he'd broken the lock on the back door, he'd had to kick aside a pile of rotten leaves that had blown in from last fall.

As he sneaked a look, he saw that she was still there, staring at the house in a way that unnerved him. He shielded his eyes from the glare of the sun off the dirty window and studied her, taking in her head of long blond hair that feathered out in the breeze from under her Western straw hat.

She wore a tan canvas jacket, jeans and boots. But it was the way she sat astride the brown-and-white horse that nudged the memory.

He felt a chill as he realized he'd seen her before. In that very spot. She'd been just a kid then. A kid on a pretty paint horse. Not this one—the markings were different. Anyway, it couldn't have been the same horse, considering the last time he had seen her was more than twenty years ago. That horse would be dead by now.

His mind argued it probably wasn't even the same girl. But he knew better. It was the way she sat the horse, so at home in a saddle and secure in her world on the other side of that fence.

To the boy he'd been, she and her horse had represented freedom, a freedom he'd known he would never have—even after he escaped this house.

Nate saw her shift in the saddle, and for a moment he feared she planned to dismount and come toward the house. With Ellis Harper in his grave, there would be little to keep her away.

To his relief, she reined her horse around and rode back the way she'd come.

As he watched her ride away, he thought about the way she'd stared at the house—today and years ago. While the smartest thing she could do was to stay clear of this house, he had a feeling she'd be back.

Finding out her name should prove easy, since he figured she must live close by. As for her interest in Harper House… He would just have to make sure it didn't become a problem.

* * * * *

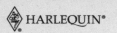
HARLEQUIN®

INTRIGUE®

WHITEHORSE MONTANA

No matter how much Nate Dempsey's past haunted
him, McKenna Bailey couldn't keep him off her mind.
He'd returned to town to bury his troubled youth—
but she wouldn't stop pursuing him until he was
working on the ranch by her side.

Look for

MATCHMAKING
WITH A
MISSION

BY

B.J. DANIELS

Available in April
wherever books are sold.

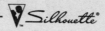

SPECIAL EDITION™

Introducing a brand-new miniseries

Men of
Mercy Medical

Gabe Thorne moved to Las Vegas to open a
new branch of his booming construction
business—and escape from a recent tragedy.
But when his teenage sister showed up pregnant
on his doorstep, he really had his hands full.
Luckily, in turning to Dr. Rebecca Hamilton for
the medical care his sister needed, he found
a cure for himself....

Starting with

THE MILLIONAIRE
AND THE M.D.

by *TERESA SOUTHWICK,*

available in April wherever books are sold.

REQUEST YOUR FREE BOOKS!
2 FREE NOVELS PLUS 2 FREE GIFTS!

SPECIAL EDITION®
Life, Love and Family!

SSE08

SAVE $1.⁰⁰

Family crises, old flames
and returning home…
Hannah Matthews and
Luke Stevens discover that
sometimes the unexpected
is just what it takes to start
over…and to heal the heart.

SHERRYL WOODS

New York Times BESTSELLING AUTHOR

SHERRYL WOODS

∽ *Seaview Inn* ∽

"Flesh-and-blood characters,
terrific dialogue and subterranial snakes…"
—*Publishers Weekly on A Slice of Heaven*

On sale March 2008!

SAVE $1.⁰⁰ on the purchase price
of SEAVIEW INN
by Sherryl Woods.

Offer valid from March 1, 2008, to May 31, 2008.
Redeemable at participating retail outlets. Limit one coupon per purchase.

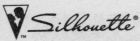

COMING NEXT MONTH